Finding My Way

By Joel H Robbins

Finding My Way

By Joel Robbins

No portion of this publication may be reproduced, stored in any electric system, or transmitted in any form or by any means, electronic, mechanical, photocopy, recording or otherwise, without the written permission of the publisher.

ISBN: 9798673610671
Copyright © 2020, 3021, 2022
Joel H Robbins

Publisher
Robbins Books
Nokomis, Florida 34275

How This Book Became About

Sara broke her hip. Surgery provided a new hip joint. She spent a week or more in a rehab hospital. I was keeping friends and King's Gate Club residents up to date through Facebook posts.

After she passed, I busied myself with silly posts about living without Sara.

v

TOUGH YEARS FOR SARA

Shingles, thumb surgery, heart attack, scleroderma, neck surgery, other pains. Plus, she never got completely back from the hip replacement. She had about one good day at home with me before a bowel blockage sent her back to a hospital. She's basically having chemicals and machines keeping her alive. I was there yesterday, and she hardly moved, only opened her eyes when I called her name, but I don't think she recognized me. I've come down with a sore throat so only called to the doctor today. She's still on life support.

It's going to be a long time before she is able to function normally, and there's lots of pain now and to come. I'm praying, but I think she's more ready to move on that I am. She has been miserable for years. Right now, I'm a mess too. She's been my life for 60 years so far.

What is our purpose in life? Well, she fulfilled it all and more. You keep yourself healthy, get a good education, marry the love of your life, have children, help them become independent, watch them have children of their own, serve your God, make the world a better place, bring joy to the people around you and, as many of the love songs croon about--grow old together. In short, love and be loved. What more can we ask for in one life?

I'm still hoping for a miracle.

LAST WORDS

As many of you know, Sara's had a series of medical conditions these past few years. She never completely returned to normal from the trauma of shingles, thumb surgery, scleroderma, a heart attack and stents.

Then she fell, broke her hip. She was in rehab until last week after hip surgery, released with home care and getting PT. The opioids she has been on for years because of neck, hip and back pain, plus those from post-surgery, caused this latest ailment, bowel obstruction and perforated bowel.

Sara passed today. I believe she was ready. She always had this saying she got from granddaughter Remy when Remy, as a little girl, was in time-out. When some little silly thing didn't go right, Sara would turn to me with a fake frown and say in a little girl's voice: "I'm not happy anymore."

I was with her when they rolled her into surgery to remove most of her large colon. She turned her head and I tilted mine so that we were looking directly into each other's eyes. She said, "Goodbye." I hesitated and lifted my eyebrows. She knew that wasn't what I expected—*see you in a little bit, or love you, honey, or sorry for being so much trouble.* She always apologized for troubles to others that weren't her fault. So, she stared at me more intently and repeated calmly, but with emphasis, "Goodbye."

Those were her last words. I didn't comprehend them until a day later. She never regained consciousness.

My favorite work of Sara's was painted at Peggy's Cove. A couple, who we were traveling with through Nova Scotia, and I took in the sights there, then went on to tour Halifax. Sara's artist's eyes were so full she stayed behind, set up her easel, watercolors and folding chair. By herself all day with God and man's glorious handiwork in front of her, she probably did some of her finest paintings.

Well, for months she has said, "I'm not happy anymore," in that half kidding/half serious voice. I'd chuckle at the inside joke. I know she misses her family and friends, but I hope, now that she's passed and in a better place, she's painting watercolors and saying, "I'm happy again."

LESSONS

Now that Sara is gone, I'm starting to learn a lot. We have a clothes washer and dryer in a closet. I guess it's been there all the time. I also realize that every house we've lived in was hers; she just let me have half the bed if she was happy with me and a lumpy sofa if she wasn't. Me telling her she would be sleeping on the couch? Never happened!

In our house up north, because of furniture, there was hardly room on the floor to wrestle with the kids or dog. If we had races through the house or played pitch and catch with a football, some of her paintings, plates and other decorations were knocked off the wall. We thought, so what? Just a wall decoration. But every piece had a history and our punishment was to stand there, chins on chests and the dog's tail between its hind legs, and hear all the details about Aunt Thelma's carnival glass dish or Grandma Stoops's miniature pitcher collection.

As the kids moved out, she spread some of her heirlooms and painting supplies into a basement play/TV room. I set up a home office to begin my journalism career after retiring from teaching. It had been our daughter's then our son's bedroom. I was so proud because she told me I had it all to myself--until one day she had me tote in her desk and more paintings, furniture and craft items.

She periodically rearranged everything on MY side of the office to make things more handy for ME. She was a woman and women have to have their husbands move furniture around as soon as hubby gets comfortable with the way it was. I could never find my reference books, printer cartridges, phone book, printer paper and wastebasket. But she always explained again how much handier it was for me.

When she took over our dining room table for scrapbooking, she asked if I minded. Then she took over the shed. I built a garage and she started to fill it up, using my work bench. She took over the back of the basement and then her projects gravitated into the kid's former play/TV room in the front of the basement.

When we bought our house in King's Gate, I asked if the furniture, draperies, carpet, kitchen, and wall colors were to her liking. If there was something she didn't like, we'd look at another furnished house in the club. I didn't want to buy a place and completely remodel and refurnish it. What a silly question to pose to your wife. As soon as the papers were signed, she pulled the feathers of the former female out of each room one at a time like a spring robin returning to take over another bird's last year's nest. Over the years Sara re-feathered our nest with new windows, window coverings, chairs, flooring, shower, kitchen counters, appliances, wall colors, pillows, hand thrown pottery and paintings, lots of paintings.

She had a walk-in closet, the master bedroom and a bathroom twice the size of ours up north. I had the guest bedroom and a tiny bathroom with a 1980s peach colored counter and a toilet paper dispenser out of reach. She wanted to remodel it. I lied and said I loved the peach counter and having to get up to unroll the TP.

I know some of you will think this bit of comedy is in bad taste with her death still fresh in your minds, but I've always been a joke teller. We started dating when she was 14 and I was 17, a sophomore and a senior. That was 1961. We've been in love for 59 years. She loved my sense of humor, and I loved that she laughed at my jokes even when they weren't funny.

Did all this housekeeping bother me? Not really. When she took over a section of the living room, easel and all, to paint watercolors, I'd think of one of my favorite plays, "You Can't Take It with You." Every family member in the play had a different passion, so the house was in a constant state of chaotic pleasure. I told Sara: "As long as it makes you happy and fulfills your creative spirit, do it, because you can't take it with you, Honey."

In "Our Town," Thornton Wilders has his characters say,

EMILY (who has passed): "Does anyone ever realize life while they live it... every, every minute?"

STAGE MANAGER: "No. Saints and poets maybe...they do some."

I think Sara was both a saint and a poet.

I miss her terribly.

TRYING TO CHANGE THE SUBJECT

An anonymous FB friend suggested I change the subject of my posts, since everyone who knew me before Sara passed already was aware that I was helpless and hopeless. I'll try to not digress, but I've mentioned her already. And, hey, she kept me organized. Every day she'd give me a to-do list, and now I'm not only helpless and hopeless but listless too. Makes me feel lazy.

I'm still getting used to the kitchen. Sara always liked to be decorative, so she collected about two dozen or more green bottles. She always poured kitchen cooking liquids out of their original containers into these bottles and lined them up on the windowsill above the sink. I get tired of plain diet coke and I didn't have any lemon, wild cherry or vanilla cola on hand, so I thought I would make my own 'mixed' drink. I started opening corks and sniffing all the way through the lineup. Biden would have been proud of me. There were many: white vinegar, cider vinegar, olive oil, corn oil (I think), and Crayola oil, vanilla, and coconut oil. I opened the coke can and poured from the vanilla bottle. It tasted good. I went to my mailbox and my neighbor Richard was getting his mail too. He looked at me and asked, "Are you okay, Joel? You're foaming at the mouth."

I went inside to the mirror, sure enough, I was blowing bubbles with each breath. Some nice ones that I bounced around the bathroom. After I'd popped a dozen bubbles, I looked around the kitchen and then under the kitchen sink to find the culprit, vanilla scented Palmolive dish soap. And I always thought that Palmolive was palm and olive scented.

Went shopping again yesterday even being listless—I wasn't maskless, though. Working on my keto die, I went right to the meat counters stalking big game. I bought some extra-long franks but smallish when it comes to wild game. Since baseball has been suspended, I thought I'd blacken a few in the oven until they were ballpark shriveled, bun them, slather mustard on top, then twist my hat around backward and watch reruns of the World Series. Anyway, I didn't recognize most of the cuts in the meat case, let alone the animal they came from. So, I just bought cut-lets, since that sounded like cute, or little, cuts of meat.

I needed some sausage patties but didn't know which brand to buy. There was Morning Visitor, Ickieridge Farm, or Kountry Kitchen. I rejected Morning Visitor, a little too personal and forward, Ickier-idge Farm sounded icky, and Kountry Kitchen bothered me because if you can't spell country then I'm not trusting you with my ground-up pork parts. Finally, I eyed Jimmy Dean fresh sausage patties. I liked him in "Rebel without a Cause" and "Giant," so I chose those. A lady next to me was looking over my shoulder. "Great singer, wasn't he?" I just rolled my eyes.

WASHER

　　Filled the washer again, but this time found the clothes washing soap. Last time I just threw in a mostly used bar from the shower and let her rip. So, I looked for the requisite measuring scoop. There were all sizes. I picked the plastic one with a spoon on each end. It looked a little like the one I use to fill my reusable Keurig cups. One end was probably a teaspoon and the other a tablespoon. Hey, I took chemistry and home ec. I chose the tablespoon.

　　Now, where to put it. There was a tunnel in the post sticking up in the center. Nope. How about the triangular opening at the outside edge. Don't know. Then I grabbed the lid to a rectangle door and a long screen came out. It had the coolest bluish-gray fabric on it. I think it's too flimsy to use as a dish rag, though. But it was fun to play with. Confused, I just tossed a tablespoon full of the soap on the clothes and shut the lid.

　　I'm still befuddled by the row of knobs and indicators across the washer that continues along the top of the dryer. Why doesn't the washer just have a GO button, and the dryer have a GO AGAIN button. Why make wash-n-dry so complicated!

　　If I wanted to learn to fly by instruments, I would have gone to a flight simulator. I needed a copilot and a checklist like they use for preflight.

    1] Load size? A) Heavy   B) medium   C) tiny.
     MEDIUM. Check.
   2] Finish?
    A) wrinkle free
    B) puckered?
     WRINKLE FREE. Check.
   3] Temperature?
    A) hot
    B) warm
    C) luke warm
    D) chilly
    E) ice cubes?
     LUKE WARM. Check.
   4]Type?
    A) Permapress
    B) delicates
    C) semidry
    D) dry

E) sunny side up
F) once over lightly?
DRY. Check.

I'm learning that the washer and dryer are magicians. I had folded and stuffed bunches of white socks into individual wads to fashion small "basketballs." I like to lie in bed with a bucket on my dresser and shoot "baskets." Well when I was stuffing my jeans, towels, colored T-shirts, boxers and socks into the washer, I forgot to unfold the socks. After washing and drying, I was taking the clothes out of the dryer and found that one projectile had turned into what looked like a white, felt, heavy ball. Cool. Bigger than a tennis ball. All the others came out partially un-wadded.

I was a little surprised when my red T-shirt came out pale pink, and my white boxers were pinkish. In fact, there was a tint of pink in the towels and socks too. I rushed to the bathroom mirror to see if I was infected with pink eye. No. I'm OK.

Sara always folded my clothes neatly and placed them in my dresser or bathroom cabinet. I tried that and nothing came out square. The fractious "folded" towels all ended up different sizes and shapes. So, I just folded a bath towel in fourths, placed a flat washcloth on it, then topped that with a hand towel folded double— again, bath towel, washcloth and hand towel, bath towel, washcloth and hand towel. Clever, hey?

The problem is when I want a bath towel and there's a washcloth and a hand towel on top of it. Yank. My cabinet is now an octagon of Mixed Martial Terrycloth. I didn't even try with my socks and T-shirts; I just wadded them up and stuffed them in drawers.

LAUNDRY

Where is all of this washing coming from? I counted 28 pairs of boxers. I think there's been another man living in the crawl space. How many undies does one man need, 3 or 3 ½ pair a week? And folding laundry is for the birds but, since I'm from the Robins species, I guess that's my burden in life. Question: Why do my undershorts come out of the dryer with the fly in the rear? If I forget to turn them around before I put them on, it's like being in a hospital gown—breezy.

I didn't know that washed and dried clothes were spooky, but when I pull a T-shirt out of the jumble of dry clothes, sometimes the hair on my forearms stands at attention. Then a hankie will get lost; I find it stuck to my chest and I have to peel it off.

Someone texted me that the felt balls I found in the dryer aren't white gym socks that have bonded and become BFF. They fluff up the clothing. Cool. I took two and decided to play with the cat. She loves it when I throw a ping pong ball into the bathtub—around and around, lap after lap, until she gets dizzy and falls over. It's cute. I figured the felt balls would be something she could literally get her claws into. So, I called Blue, who was asleep on the sofa. She looked up and I threw a ball and let it roll past her. She looked at it and then at me.

"Fetch."

Now that I could see she was ready, I threw another one. She went back to sleep. I want a dog.

Hey, what's with the socks! I put in 4 pairs, 2 different colors, and I took out 3 black ones, 1 white one and 1 light green one. Take your eyes off these rascals for a few hours and they think they're feet instead of socks and walk off, saying, "I know how this is done. I've got a lot of close friends that are feet? We've taken a lot of walks together." And where did the tiny green one come from? I think when I closed the dryer door some hanky-panky took place.

COOKIES

I know, I said I ended the series on coping without Sara. But because of requests from an overwhelming number of Facebook readers, well actually, only 2, here is another. But, it will be the last last posting of its kind.

I've been trying a keto diet, so I've avoided carbs. But I broke down the other day because I was craving cookies. I scouted the kitchen and found Sara's recipes. One of my favorites was the Muncie Fair cookie winner of 1939.

Not just wanting one ordinary puny cookie, I started thinking. Sara always got after me when I would grab a half dozen cookies from the cooling racks, pour a glass of milk and head for the lanai.

"How many cookies did you take? Six empty spots! JOEL! That's ridiculous!" (Sara spoke with a lot of exclamation points.)

"No, it's not. I would have taken more if my hands were bigger!"

So, I decided to make a Joel-sized cookie. Then, with Sara looking down at me from above, I could say, "See, I only ate one cookie."

I figure that instead of a 3-inch-across cookie, I'd go for 12 inches. Being a math genius, I decided I'd better triple the recipe.

I looked at the recipe card and tripled it:

4 C. sugar (half brown) became 12 C. sugar

1 C. lard and a stick of butter became 3 C. Crisco and 3 sticks of butter

2 t. Baking Soda became   6 c. baking soda

3 t. vanilla became   9 tablespoons of vanilla

½ t. salt became 3 tablespoons of salt, I rounded up the measurement because I don't do fractions

6 C. Flour became 18 c. flour

4 eggs beaten became a dozen eggs

I had some problems:
1. No lard, but I found Crisco
2. Couldn't find any cup measures, so I used a coffee mug
3. I had to go buy more flour and Crisco

4.

5. The only baking soda container in the kitchen was open and, in the refrigerator, hard as dried plaster of Paris. So, I remembered seeing a big-box-store-sized box in the pantry. It was so big it had a plastic carrying strap. I thought that baking soda was white but this was gray. It wasn't powdery, more like Grape Nuts cereal, not the
flakes, similar to ground volcanic rock. Oh, well, what do I know? Glad I found a large box; it would have taken many of the small ones to add up to 6 cups.

6. Didn't find a 5 lb. sack of brown sugar, so I browned some white sugar on the stove. The first few batches turned black, and one caught on fire.

7. When I started pouring the ingredients into the glass bowl, I saw I was in trouble. It was full right away. So, I washed out a bucket from the shed.

8. Sara would use this wire thing the shape of a light bulb to beat eggs. That's usually when I quit watching, because 'why stick around if the cookies wouldn't be ready for an hour.' Anyway, I beat the eggs (felt bad about that) and then added the rest of the ingredients. The wire light bulb couldn't take it, and I discarded the tangled wire in the wastebasket. I had to finish with my portable drill and a 3-bladed stirrer for a 5 gallon paint can. I shouldn't have used high speed. (I need to make a note to scrape clean the ceiling.)

The mixture was beautiful and smelled great. I punched broil and 425 degrees to preheat the oven. Then I remembered, I'm "baking" cookies not "broiling" steaks. I switched to bake. I patted out my Joel-sized cookie on the counter, and, since I couldn't find the cookie sheets, it went on aluminum foil. Man, I was proud of myself.

Just as the cookie, all toasty brown and delicious smelling, was cool enough to eat, my buddy Rod walked in.

Rod: "Wow! That smells good. You bake that?"

Me: "Yep. Good timing, pal."

"What's the cat litter doing in the kitchen?"

"That's not cat litter, silly, that's baking soda. Says Arm & Hammer right there on the orange box. The Tidy Cat is in the bathroom with the litter box. I'm taking a bite."

"Well, how's it taste?"

"It's yummy but kind of clumping in my throat."

"That's because it says 'clumping' right on the box, Joel."

"Yeah, I saw that, so I took the warning and mixed longer than I thought required."

"You okay! You look a little pale."

"I'm having a little trouble swallowing. Do you know how to apply the Heimlich maneuver?"

SNACKS

Now that Sara's not around to pick up after me, my life has changed. For one thing, I used to find a new episode of "Forged in Fire," fix a bowl of popcorn, and watch. Other times my primetime snack was red-skinned Spanish peanuts—no offense to Native Americans or swarthy Spaniards. A family-size bag of taco flavored Dorita's went down easily, too, many evenings. A box of Sun-Maid raisins provided some late-night fruit snacks, and, of course, MMs. All healthy items to munch on, right, I'd tell Sara? She'd give me one of those looks. Well, I'd counter, "They all have to be on the USDA Food Pyramid somewhere."

Instead of just one type of snack, now I can reach between the cushions of the sofa for a "variety pack" of treats. It provides some mystery. It's like a GORP if you get a handful. I used to backpack occasionally, and I always took GORP, but I could never remember what the acronym meant. Grapes, Onions, Radishes and Prunes? Ooh, wouldn't that provide an olfactory surprise in a double sleeping bag being Dutch ovened. I think I just verbed a noun.

Coming out of high school I weighed 170. Out of college, 180. After teaching one year and eating high school cafeteria food, 220. Then summers I worked construction, 190. Winters teaching, 220. Summers, 190, winters teaching, 220. In my middle 60s, I lived in Azerbaijan while serving in the peace Corps and walked everywhere, 185. Moved to King's Gate Club, 230.

So, I have been culling the snacks that Sara had hidden all over the house. If she left them out, each time I passed the counter I ate one, let's say a cookie. What's one cookie! Well, take that times 27 trips through the kitchen. That's a lot of Oreos! If she hid them in drawers and cabinets, every time she left the house to go to an evening meeting I'd burrow through her dresser to uncover a bag of MM peanuts, maple nut goodies, juju beans, red licorice, or Snicker minis.

She wouldn't be home more than 15 minutes before she would come onto the lanai, bend down with hand on her thigh and her hip cocked to one side, and ask: "Why in heaven's name have you been in my bra and panties' drawer?"

Head between my knees, I'd squeak out, "I missed you?"
"Right!"
"Ok, I could smell those maple nut goodies!"
"OMG, Joel." She started stashing most things in her master bathroom. Yeah, she had the master bathroom and I had the mistress bathroom. That wasn't right.

She had to hide the crackers, peanut butter, granola bars, gummy bears and anything else with salt, sugar and shovelfuls of carbs. Visitors for wine and cheese always looked on with wrinkled brows as I went to the kitchen for the cheese and Sara went to her bathroom and brought out boxes of crackers.

Wine was the same. People would ask, "What do you do with a half full bottle of opened wine?"

Answer: "What's that?"

She hid the wine too. If it sat on the counter, as with the snacks, I'd fill my glass every time I walked by until life became a little confusing. Baileys and blackberry brandy were a double temptation, sugar high and alcohol buzz all in one. I finally found that she hid those under her mattress pad and slept curled around them so that she wouldn't wake up in the middle of the night to catch me tiptoeing out of her bathroom in my boxers with a bottle in each hand.

CREAMS

Sara: "You're not going out like that, are you!"

Me: "Well, I have pants on and they're zipped. That's pretty well done for a 76-year-old man."

"Change that shirt."

"Why?"

"Change that shirt."

Then I would come out with a different flowered shirt on and she'd say, "Your collars turned up."

I'd lie and say, "I want it that way."

"You're not Elvis, turn down your collar."

I never knew why. I just had to change my shirt and put my collar down.

It was kind of like when she would stop talking to me.

"What's wrong, Honey."

"I'm not talking about it."

"Then how can I fix it?"

"You heard me, we're not talking about it."

A preacher friend of mine told me what he does when that happens to him. He said he buys his wife a bouquet of flowers, comes home, gives them to her and says, "I'm so sorry, Dear. It'll never happen again."

BINGO!

Life with a woman is mysterious.

When we'd sit on the lanai for coffee, Sara continually said, "Look at your legs."

"Why? I'm not attracted to men's legs."

"Put some cream on them."

Okay, they looked dry, but my masculinity disappeared as I rubbed body lotion up and down my legs.

Recently, I was looking for some of that lotion and searched in Sara's cabinets. Glory be! I'd hit the motherlode. I hoped we had stock in Bath & Body Works. There was one just to heal the heels. With it was an egg-shaped object reminiscent of Easter. I tried the side that looked like a cheese grater on my callused heel and parmesan sifted to the floor. With the leather on the other side I buffed my dress shoes.

Another cream was for the elbows. A salve promised to clear up cracked hands. One square metal can contained a yellowish, thick substance. The label on top read "Bag balm." Really! Then I looked at the front of the can and it pictured a cow, and on one side it read: "Udder-ly soothing." Okay, got it. But why did we have it?

There was face cream, body lotion, hand lotion, cosmetic removal cream, anti-itch cream, triple-antibiotic cream, suntan lotion, Brylcreem, analgesic lotion and Anti-Wrinkle Magic. I used the later on that wrinkled flowered shirt, but no luck, still lots of creases. I can't wear that shirt now, thank you very much. The hemorrhoidal cream I kept. I read that it shrinks the bags under your eyes. I tried it on the right eye, while the left eye volunteered as a control subject. Plus, I wanted a before and after image. The cream was effective. The right eye looked normal, but people kept asking me if I had a sty under the other.

In her bathroom, I hesitated, took a deep breath of perfumed air, Oh Sara, I miss you!

Continuing on my hunt, I opened another drawer of creams. It was like being in a tropical plantation: l'essence de pineapple, citrus, jasmine, roses, banana, kumquat, cinnamon apple Jamaican cheesecake, etc. Then there was "oile e pollein de l'hay." I took a hefty sniff. Yep, back on the farm. Since I know that many of these products resemble Crisco, Valvoline, olive oil, suet and sheep lanolin, I kept looking for a gallon of 409 Degreaser. Then I started sneezing uncontrollably.

THE PANTRY

Well, I told you I found a clothes washer and dryer in a closet the other day. Been there all along. Today I found the food pantry. It's like a mini-mart--potatoes in a sack on the floor sprouting roots. That was cool. Softish extremely aromatic onions in a fishnet bag. Didn't know that was what Sara did with her old hose. Then an open box of raisins that contain something I swear I've seen in a sheep pasture, a bottle of rice wine (not *sake,* I tried it) for cooking(?), and a flat can of crab meat. What's that for?

I scooted the wastebasket next to the shelves and started tossing items, things such as open bags of croutons half-filled with small chunks that looked like objects you might pick up in a limestone driveway. Harder, though. When I found three plastic containers of three different flavors of Betty Crocker icings, I scurried to the silverware drawer and grabbed three spoons. Then I looked at my belly and did a forehead slap and put the containers in a Publix tote to get them out of sight.

I turned on 195 to see if KGC was still collecting for a food pantry. Yes, # 10 Castle Drive, the Bakeovens. Salvation!

Returning to the pantry, I found Marsala de Guarnizione in a bottle, one of the Guarnizione sisters made it, I guess. Into more totes went two, squat jars of mealie paste labeled pesto. It looked like ground pests, flies or ants maybe, in oil, so it's understandable how they arrived at the name. Why did we have that? We had never had goldfish to feed. There were three sealed, blue, square, flat enevlopes of smoked salmon and tuna. I guess Sara received those envelopes in the mail as samples.

Two cans said coconut milk. Didn't know you could milk a coconut. I can't believe all the things I'm learning. One half gallon plastic bottle was Sunsweet prune juice. I handled that with care cause that much in one place might be explosive.

I realized that poor Sara scrimped in some ways. We had several cans, large and small, of mushroom stems and pieces. I guess she thought we couldn't afford two buy whole mushrooms. Chicken broth, chicken and noodle soup, chicken of the sea, chicken broth gravy, chicken flavored Ramen Noodles and one large container advertised "a whole chicken" in a can. We had chickens when I was a kid, I'd like to have seen them pulling that off. Anyway, somewhere chickens are having a bad day.

CABINET

If you're alone and hear an otherworldly sounding voice telling you to get Joel psychiatric help, it's probably just Sara yelling down from above.

Moving on. You have to be bored it you voluntarily stick your head among the dangerous jetsam and flotsam under your bathroom sink. It was time to sort and toss the old tubes, bottles, boxes, floss and moss. I preferred pulling out the jetsam, because flotsam elicited an unsavory image, especially if you've ever swum in a pool with a lot of small children.

Just the wafts of air in that cave of chemicals and cosmetics made me a little woozy. Right away I found a cream for a tropical fungus. I used to place that tube front and center on the eye-level shelf with my pills. Snooping visitors, using the bathroom, I hoped would look in horror at globs of Vicks I dabbed on it and close the cabinet and quit prying into my private life.

Of course, there were bottles with labels peeled off. Dates in the last century. And iodine, merthiolate and Mercurochrome. As a kid, those were my 'red badge of courage' with other kids. I'd ask Mom to use that little glass applicator to spread it out all over my elbow, not just on the cut.

I found a Johnson & Johnson box of little round Band-aids. Yeah, I need pimple covers at 76. Admit it, though, pimples were horrifying but fun. What teen hasn't enjoyed an hour with head cocked to one side and one bulging eye almost touching the mirror, while two index fingers closed in on a cheek bump that had a white summit. Then with a half dozen squeezes, he turned a peaceful snowcapped mountain into a fiery-looking volcano--lava flowing.

I took a break for lunch then went to the pantry I had cleaned out the day before. Surprise, a whole stack of gourmet pate I had not seen. There were little cans that looked like tuna cans containing seafood delights of every kind. They even had easy-open ring tops.

I like shrimp, I like pate, I have crackers, I'm ready for a Fancy Feast. That was the brand name. I found the cat really like them too. She wouldn't leave me alone to enjoy my pate on a Ritz with a half of pimento-filled olive on top. I lifted each cracker in one hand with one pinky extended and held a can of beer in my other. That's upper class!

If you stacked the pate carefully you could get one entire can on one club cracker. I tried the savory salmon, tasty tuna, sea fresh sole, Cape Town cod and ocean whitefish. I'm going to have a Fancy Feast for several days because I must have 21 cans left.

Back under the bathroom cabinet I found I had to make important decisions about:

Diaper rash ointment—may need that after a vigorous shuffleboard match, kayaking or if I join a bicycling club.

Dozens of bottles or packets of Imodium—needed at the Capital Building, Washington, DC. Make note to send immediately for BS outbreak.

Aloe vera—I had a neighbor Vera once that I used to yell 'aloe' to. "Aloe, Vera."

Tube of Mentholatum—save in memory of the 1950s then google to see what it is.

Hadacol—a supposed vitamin supplement in the 1950s that was popular because it was 12% alcohol.

My head had cleared during lunch, but I almost swooned again from the reek of isopropyl alcohol, blue colored astringent, a brown bottle of hydrogen peroxide and pineapple essential oil. Knocking my head on the drainpipe periodically made me dizzier.

The place was a chemistry lab. There was boric acid, trichloroacetic acid, citric acid, amino acid, salicylic acid and an old bottle of stomach acid left over from Cinco de Mayo. I should really toss that.

LANAI

If you've ridden a horse, you may know the desperation of being thrown, which damages to your dignity, and then having the horse run away. Adding insult to injury. My house, that's right, house not horse, has thrown me and is heading for the horizon. Yesterday, for example, a friend called and said he was stopping by, so I looked around the house as if I were a visitor walking in the door. Sara always said that's how you prepare for company. Crap! I've seen cleaner chicken coops.

I decided I'd corral my friend on the lanai, because that's the smallest area. Sara resumed smoking the last few years, only on the lanai, so the room had the odor of an old-time pool hall. I searched for the Febreze, but I could only find the breeze part when I opened two windows to air it out. Wait! There's a candle that Sara always lit. I unscrewed the metal lid and saw three wicks sticking out of the purple wax. In seconds, the room smelled of gooseberries and plum. Aaaah. Well, more like scorched gooseberries and plum with a cigar butt put out in the wax.

Then I looked at all four chairs. They had grown hair. Blue's hair. I scampered to get the hand vacuum, attached a mustache-brush-looking thing to the opening and started on the furniture. An hour later I emptied the hopper. Either I swept up two dead mice from among the pillows or Blue had shed a couple of mouse-loads of black fur.

I found only one drunk-on-Home Defense cockroach on the floor. As in the cartoons, he was on his back with teeny feet pedaling. I grabbed him with my hand. Since the little legs running on my palm freaked me out, I rid myself of him as quickly as possible into the toilet. I kind of felt sorry for him as I watched him do the backstroke from one side of the bowl to the other. Flush, spiral waterslide, into the pool's dark tunnel—a Disney Land ride for an insect's last thrill.

The kitchen was a mess because I cook everything on high heat. Often grease spits clear to the ceiling. If Sara prepared stir fry with rice, she used a chopping board, two bowls, a rice cooker, two fry pans--one for the meat and one for the vegetables--and four assorted utensils. It took an hour and a half. When she asked me to cook fried rice/stir fry, the meal was on our plates in a half hour using only a herculean fry pan and a burger flipper. She liked mine better. Maybe it was because she didn't want to cook and was scamming me. Since I use few kitchen tools, why are both sinks full and the counters stacked with pans?

    I use sheets and sheets of paper towels and Kleenex. Sara used a lot of Kleenex too, which I still find stuffed between pillows, in her old robe sleeves, in the crack of the sofa, inside hoodie pockets and next to her computer. I've been discovering these droppings all over the house and car and throwing them away. Now when I walk past our many wastebaskets, they look like a gigantic wicker vanilla ice cream cone with whipped cream foaming out of and over the top. I'm going to have to empty the wastebaskets sometime next week. Even when I plunge my foot into them, the trash just springs it back violently.

    Some of the items next to where she sat on the lanai are a mystery. There was a half dozen tongue depressors that felt like sandpaper. Better to grasp the tongue? I put them in my shop for detailed woodwork. A package held green, tiny hair picks with a thread strung between two prongs. Slingshot for a squirrel? I tossed them on top of the whipped cream stuff. Then there were several colorful soft foam items next to the nail polish. SpongeBob's toes after his foot had been chomped flat by a giant clam? I dropped them on top of the hair picks.

    My friend galloped in and out without commenting on my barn-cleaning etiquette. Great! Now I won't have to straighten up the house again until the next person calls to visit.

CAT VOMIT

I can't find the things I need, and the things I do find I don't need. Did I repeat myself? Anyway, the cat hunted down a palmetto bug (that's what proud people call a cockroach), played with it, then ate it. Blue doesn't meow--she does wheeze, though, bordering on a soft snore, when she sleeps--but no sound otherwise. Unless she's about to vomit. Then it's like a screech owl in heat.

She must have gotten one of the cockroach's legs caught in her throat. When she's sick she always runs to me, like "Hey Joel, something nasty is coming up, catch it so it doesn't get on the floor. I'm proud too." If I'm in my office I quickly close the door and turn on some music, while she makes noises (elk, yak, ecru, sac, luge) in the hallway. I get queasy when I hear someone vomiting, but the rap music that comes on isn't much better. I push the ear pods further in anyway and pop a Tum.

Of course, an hour later, maybe after a short nap, I open the door, take one step in my bare feet, hit a slick spot, zip across the hall and smash into the wall like a hockey player being slammed into the boards. I walk on one good foot and tip toe on one sticky foot into the shower and wash, put on socks, then look for a mop.

Where the mops should be in the pantry there aren't any housecleaning tools I recognize. There's a broomstick with nothing on the end. Another stick has two, red floppy-ear things at one end. Hinged together. Where's the mop with the long cornrowed gray hair? Where's the yellow sponge with the built-in metal squeezer thing?

Anyway, I find a pouch-like rag nearby that looks like it might go on the rabbit ears. It's got a hole, so I stuff the plastic rabbit ears in. I wet the rag by sticking the covered rabbit ears down into the kitchen sink, only breaking one fluorescent light bulb with the handle scraping around on the ceiling.

I find about five slick, ecru-colored spots of different heights and viscosities, one with a cockroach leg sticking out, and start using the mop. It flops a lot and I end up kind of pushing it like a V-shaped snowplow. Blue, licking a paw, watches me nonchalantly, so I brandish the mop handle at her menacingly and she runs behind the sofa but still watches. She knows! I shame her by relating aloud that when I had dogs, they'd clean up after themselves. She doesn't seem surprised, probably thinking, "I'd believe that about dogs."

Later, I told a neighbor about my troubles and she told me to get a Schiffer, or something like that. Maybe that's the product with which Adam Schiff made his fortune. Of course, she could have said Swifter, named such because it works faster. For one moist spot, I just use one socked foot then toss the sock into the wastebasket—creating one more potentially mismatched pair.

When I was putting the handles back into the pantry, I came upon a fortunate discovery. Sara kept lots of her baking goods in there on the shelves. In the back on the floor she must have spilled some of the chocolate sprinkles she used on cakes and cookies. That's probably why so many palmetto bugs scurry out when I open the door. They most likely savor them too. I notice the bottle of sprinkles is only half full, so I sweep up the ones on the floor, blow off the dust and fill the bottle. I look at the window in the door to see if anyone is peaking in, then sneak a few into my mouth. They must be the bitter dark chocolate sprinkles.

THE SAGA CONTINUES

I've moved on to cleaning out the large side-by-side refrigerator and freezer. I started digging in and finally got to the back. You know, it's cold in that freezer. And very dark with the door closed like that. Tight and claustrophobic. I had to eventually push the door open with my foot, wedging it to keep it ajar so that I could see and not get hypothermia.

I found what I believed to be hamburger patties. They were mostly brown like they'd already been fried. But when I thawed them, slapped one on a bun, it didn't taste fried. Kind of soggy and red in the middle. Rancid dishcloth smell. I had trouble finishing the sandwich. It took extra ketchup, mustard and pickles.

In the bottom drawer of the freezer were four bags of rhubarb. Really! In Florida! I remember in the Gresham Hotel in Dublin seeing fresh, chopped, raw rhubarb on the breakfast buffet. The reason given was the Irish don't like sticky sweet things in the morning. No pecan rolls or glazed donuts for them. So strawberry jam is out and sour orange marmalade is in. The only way I like rhubarb is in pie: crust, top and bottom, filling made with two pads of butter, two tablespoons of flour, four cups of diced rhubarb and five cups of sugar.

Clear at the bottom of the freezer, it appeared that California blend had had a party. Very nondiscriminatory affair. Don't know if the fugitives were from one bag or a variety of frozen vegetable bags. The fugitives obviously had overwhelmed the guards, because there was a jumble of dead plastic clothes pins nearby.

A container in the back of the bottom of the refrigerator had peanut butter in it. It was dated, but most of the numbers were fuzzy and undecipherable. Only a 19 was left. It couldn't have been 1998, or something like that. So, I assumed it was last year, 2019.

Sara had written "ham" on the cover. I scooped some out onto two slices of spinach bread that I didn't know we had. It was also down there and in the back. I've seen green vegetable chips and spinach noodles, but this green bread was a new one. It had the fragrance of a Florida swamp, fecund.

Anyway, I slathered some raspberry jelly on top of the peanut butter to make a PBJ sandwich and ate some. Something had been off with Jiffy when they had made that. My daughter told me she thought it really had been ham, once a long, long time ago. I took several more bites to make sure it tasted bad before I was convinced.

Some sticky gel was pooled below the bottom drawer. It was the color of an olive but smelled like vinegar mixed with light Karo syrup. It peeled right off looking like a fruit roll-up, though, when I used a hamburger flipper. Finally done.

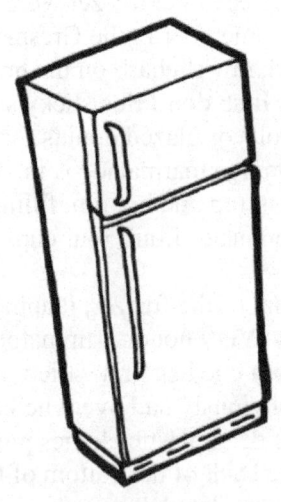

SHEETS

Someone's sneaking into my house at night. I get up and there are dishes, cups, forks, spoons and glasses on the counters in the kitchen, on the tables on the lanai and on the TV tray next to my La-Z-Boy. Plus, there's popcorn litter around my chair. I don't remember having popcorn last night. Of course, there are lots of things I don't remember, like my Post-Its of reminders. And my popcorn bowl has a thin, round, salty pad of butter at the bottom. That never happened before. I'd get up in the morning, wobble to the kitchen, get my coffee and shuffle on out to have coffee with Sara on the lanai. There were no messes. I need a security camera to see who's coming in to watch Netflix's Joe Exotic, eat my popcorn, then have a midnight snack of my Apple Fruit Loops.

Another thing that never happened before is the smell of my bedroom. One day I came home from a walk in the fresh air and went into my bedroom to hang up my sweaty shirt. When I passed the three T-shirts from the past few days hanging on pegs, it reminded me of the time I was riding a crowded bus in Kazakhstan. I was pushed up against a 6'4" fellow in a tank top with my nose up his armpit. It was dark and hairy in there, but I couldn't move.

Anyway, the entire room had the odor of the inside of a tennis shoe and dirty socks. Of course, right then I noticed two and a half pairs of socks peeking out from under the bed as if they'd been summoned. The bed clothes, instead of the pleasant scent of fabric softener, smelled like me. Me after a grueling, vigorously contested shuffleboard match. I guess Sara must have taken down the dried T-shirts regularly. I'd have just kept wearing them if she hadn't.

All the items go into the washing machine. Hours later, I take them out and stuff the T-shirts and socks into drawers. Then I attempt to make the bed. The fitted sheet appears square, but my bed is rectangular. Interesting. I get one end fitted and pull to cover the other end. Why am I straining? I can feel an old hernia starting to say hello. After trying one way, then another way, I get out my tape measure and do some checking. The springy corners preclude exact measurements and keep letting loose of the hook on my tape end and snapping back to take a bloody chunk out of my knuckle. After I circle the bed a dozen times trying for a fit, I stop for a midmorning happy hour.

Not being a quitter, I continue with the arm wrestling match and lose. When I have the scissors open and prepared for surgery in my one hand and ahold of one corner with the other, I come to my senses and go to Target for nonfitted sheets. I thought I'd fold up the old sheet and donate it to Goodwill on my way. I'm good at origami and folding paper airplanes, but I couldn't outwit this bedsheet. Luckily, the trash can was close. At Target, the best buy on sheets is a set with Micky and Minnie prints. The young sales lady gives me a blindingly white toothpasty grin and asks if I have children or grandchildren in my house. Smart-aleck! I say that no I live alone. With a slanted grin, she counters with "ménage à trois, hey?" I laugh just to be polite, because I don't understand Russian.

Someone is also tracking in sand. I can feel the grit sticking to my bare feet. One annoying and tenaciously embedded bit is a popcorn kernel. It takes nine minutes to remove it with Sara's eyelash curlers. Hey, it was all I could find! I've got to change the locks. I go to the pantry and there's that darn floppy-eared red housekeeping tool. I slide a new cover on it and, again, V snow plow it around the house. Why isn't it like other mops—all floppy cotton braids or a T shape?

There's nasty stuff piling up ahead of the mop--some moist fur balls, Blue's ping pong balls, a toe nail or two, a push pin, a French fry that has turned into a rock-hard shoestring potato, a shriveled up sliver of peperoni, a twist tie and a gross brown smear. I can't get the smear up with the mop, so I wet a scrubby with Goo Gone and go down on my hands and metal knees. Unintentionally huffing the Goo Gone makes me a little dizzy, but I give the smear a good scrubbing for 23 minutes. Nothing. Then I look at the next plank of Pergo. It has the same smear. In fact, it's on every other plank. Head slap.

LESS CIVILIZED

I'm struggling to not regress from 59 years of a woman's civilizing effects. I caught myself drinking straight from the milk jug the other day. How did I backslide so quickly! During our marriage I often had to remind Sara that: "I'm a man." Now that sounds sexist, but I would remind myself that I let her be a woman. When, in the evening on the spur of the moment, I would say, "Honey, let's go get ice cream." She'd say: "Ok, give me a second."

I'd slap a ball cap on to cover several cowlicks that had awakened while I was lounging in my Lay-Z-Boy in front of the TV, then sit in the car for an hour. She'd come out having showered, changed clothes, fixed her hair, put on makeup, buffed her fingernails, and applied perfume. When she entered the car, she would wake me and ask me to help her finish putting in an earring or clasping a necklace. We drove to Dairy Queen, ordered at the drive through, ate our Blizzards in the car and drove home. She was a woman. I accepted that. As if I had a choice! So, my reminding her to let me be a man was fair game.

If I am eating popcorn while watching an episode of Schitt Creek, and I forgot to pick up a napkin, I smell my T-shirt, decide it won't last another day anyway and daintily blot my lips and remove the butter from my fingers. Hey, it saved a napkin. I'm ecologically woke.

I notice that when Blue hacks up a hairball I don't descend on it with an old credit card and a paper towel anymore. I let it dry a few days and remove it with a wood chisel. Then I can pick it up with my fingers. Speaking of Blue, I also wear black more often now so that her hair doesn't show on what I used to wear, khaki shorts and white T-shirts. I know, I could brush the hair off the furniture or suck it up into the hand vacuum twice a day, but then I would have to brush it off the furniture and suck it up into the hand vacuum twice a day

Why do I leave the cabinet doors open more now? I've thought about removing them. I guess it's too tiring to open them and close them every time I want something. I tried that with the freezer and produced an iceberg in the ice cube maker. I'm glad I left the wood chisel out. The open cabinet doors aren't working too well, either. I have several blunt force trauma cranial contusions in my scalp.

When I am in the kitchen cooking and need to blow my nose, I use a sheet of Bounty so that I don't have to walk 10 feet to the bathroom for Kleenex. Speaking of tissue paper, my mom could hear a piece of Kleenex drop into her toilet even if I had the door closed and she was two rooms away. When she lived in a different house after my dad died, she told me, "Joey, now my home's gastrointestinal tract has a very delicate nature. It can't digest tissue paper…………..." I wanted to say, "Mom, it's a toilet, john, crapper, not a renter with inflammatory bowel syndrome."

Sara had good hearing too:

"Joel, I didn't hear you flush twice, one a courtesy flush and then the cleansing one?"

"Courtesy flush?"

"Either that or use the floral spray right away."

"I wasn't in there with guests!"

"Joel, Joel, Joel!"

If I see a wad of paper on the floor, instead of picking it up, I tell myself that I'll leave it for Blue to bat around when she wakes up. Maybe it'll get pushed under the sofa and I won't have to think about it anymore. Blue has been out of sorts with me lately. When she leaves her litter box, she comes over and bites my bare ankle. It might just be because I've only been scooping once a week. I let the litter box crust over, then take a hammer and give it one good whack—it breaks up like peanut brittle—then I lift out chunks with cooking tongs from the kitchen and hang them back up over the toaster.

BIRD FEEDER

I put up a bird feeder a couple of months ago. A variety of birds pass my lanai windows each week: white ibises, crows, lots of mockingbirds, ground doves, cardinals, blue jays, grackles, red bellied woodpeckers, red winged blackbirds, Carolina wren, palm warblers, sandhill cranes, little blue herons, red shouldered hawks and silky ibises. It's been a religious experience.

Everyone knows that cardinals are Catholic, right? And blue jays are Presbyterian. Think about it! The cardinal is all in red vestment and the blue jay has a blue chasuble over a white alb. You know right away they have status in the heavens and on earth. Now, the common ground doves have to be the monks or brothers. They wait until everyone else has visited the feeder. They then shuffle around picking up the scraps on the ground, wearing a sandy-brown habit. Very humble and deferential. There's no pomp and circumcision about them, so we know they're not Jewish.

Speaking of Jews, I think the grackles, all in black, might be Hasidic Jews—excellent posture and sartorially prefect. The bird that does the daily ritual of ablutions, the robin, might be Muslim. The mockingbirds are either Methodist or Baptist, because they're everywhere and sing a lot. Atheists are the murders of crows, because the mockingbirds are always chasing them away. Besides, crows suck eggs, and, when other kids at school yelled across the street, "Joel sucks eggs," I never took it as a compliment.

My cat Blue is said to have nine lives, so she's either Hindu or Buddhist. What's Blues link to birds. She peers out the lanai windows at them, chattering, pawing, and drooling, except when she is catnapping. Her twitching and slapping tail sends the coasters, candles and wine glasses catapulting off the coffee table she sits on. With her fascination, I guess you could call her a catbird.

The red bellied woodpeckers pride themselves for their red caps, so they're probably MAGA Republicans. The tree-huggers (palm warblers) might be liberals. Politics and religion in one post, oops!

The seeds I put in the feeder that aren't eaten are germinating. I have a four-foot stalk of milo growing in Sara's garden. I expect field corn, peanuts, sunflowers and beans to sprout soon. Plus, they're growing directly under the feeder, meaning well fertilized with guano, which is Spanish for, well, you know.

I also learned about the idiom, "pecking order." The red winged blackbird may be at the top. Even the bully grackles make way for red winged blackbirds. The ibes or ibides (plurals for ibis) look as if they've dipped their wing tips in an inkwell. They turn their noses down at everything.

Sandhill cranes are traffic cops. At least they bring my Miata to a tire-smoking skid when they stand in the middle of King Arthur Drive with our eyes at the same level. The peace maker is the red shouldered hawk, because when he skydives below the trees and jets down the street at about bush-top level, all the birds hold still, pause their eating and stop singing. Party pooper!

DRONES

I bought two drones and took them to my son's for Christmas, hoping that they would provide an activity I could share and enjoy with my son, my 15-year old grandson, and my 12-year-old granddaughter. We had fun and I left them there for them to enjoy. Back home Rod Kent and I were talking about flying his trick kites, and I said let's get drones instead. They make their own wind. So, we did.

Mine came in first and Rod was busy, so I grabbed Ron Peltier and we went to the little KGC hall and played test pilot. I set up a tote lid as a landing pad and told him I'd give him a flying lesson. Afterall, I had flown drones with my grandkids. I was almost an expert. I missed the pad three times in a row with Ron watching. Then I let Ron try and he stuck it the first time. I was ready to take my ball and bat, I mean drone and controller, and go home.

We set up a couple of mic stands and weaved the drone between and around them. We both did fairly well until Ron ran it into the wall and the breakaway guards for the blades flew everywhere. I smiled. Now I didn't have to go home in a huff. I put the drone back together, then we placed it facing away from us. When I tapped the GO button, it decided to execute a jack-in-a-box, perform a pirouette, then go for Ron's scalp. Didn't know Ron could move that fast. Continuing, we flew it into the wall five or six times before I had an 'aha' moment, realizing something needed recalibrated. I was held back in the third grade, ya know.

I took it home and recalibrated it. The next day I took it to the soccer fields behind the croquet club on Pinebrook. I sat at a picnic table for about 20 minutes getting everything together, but it only took one minute after I pushed GO for my $90 drone to skim across the field, jump a fence and fly up into the pines or down into the bushes. I was pushing the REturn button as hard as I could. It has lights and beeps, but I couldn't fine it. Plus, I looked like I was a soda can picker, walking in fits, starts and circles peering into trees and down into the shrubbery. I went from a proud owner of a new drone to being droneless. I packed up controller, extra blades, a pack of tiny screws and an instruction manual and did the walk of shame to the car. Then I looked at the items in my hands and wondered why I was taking them home. Did I expect the drone to be sitting on my doorstep like a returned runaway puppy? I'm sure the members of the girls' soccer team that was practicing nearby looked at each other and said, "Didn't that old dude have a drone when he walked out on the field?" I refused to make eye contact when I passed several in the parking lot.

Having learned my lesson, I bought another drone two and a half times as expensive. I figured it would be automatic—fly upside down, do flips, return when I whistled, play my favorite songs and retrieve letters from the mailbox. It took me two days to understand the manual. The first line, I finally realized, was supposed to read: "Open the box, remove the drone, plug the USB cable into your computer to charge the batteries." In actuality it read: "Free chest, delete low hum, stop up USB inside computer to accuse the lithium tubes."

I watched a video about using the drone, read and reread the manual and translated the remainder of the pages from what looked like a Chinese-to-English thesaurus to proper English sentences. The correct directions said to 1) push the drone's ON button, 2) toggle the left speed lever straight up then straight down until you hear a beep and the lights flash slowly, 3) push the speed and the direction control toggles simultaneously in opposite directions until the lights flash rapidly, 4) push and hold the CALibration button until you hear beep beep, 5) turn the drone clockwise horizontally until you hear beep beep beep, 6) turn it clockwise while holding it vertically until you hear a bebop, 7) press down hard on the MOde button till your eyeballs roll back in your head, 8) swallow triple Jell-O shots to clear your head, 9) push the GO button until the propellers spin.

And spin they did, causing my expensive drone to bounce off the ceiling in rapid succession like a moth ricocheting off a hot light bulb at night. With bits of textured ceiling being sheared off with each bounce, I pushed every lever and every button on the remote. Only one worked, and that was LAnd, but it didn't turn off the propellers, which hacked at my blinds as the drone dived toward the floor. There it became stuck between a table leg and the wall.

One propelled was obstructed and, although its motor was running at mach 2, it couldn't turn. I smelled smoke, managed to avoid most of the slicing and dicing blades, and grabbed the drone. I turned it off at the expense of only one bloodied finger. The propeller that hadn't been spinning had an oily vapor threading out of it and rising to the ceiling. I set the drone down and pinched the motor that was smoking to see if it was hot. I heard a sizzle, smelled a fried pork chop and stuck my thumb and index finger in my mouth. I was also held back in the seventh grade.

STILL DRONING AND GROANING

Having learned my lesson, I ordered a new drone.

Icarus had hubris, ignored Father Daedalus and flew too close to the sun, melting the waxed-in feathers. He fell, crashed, and burned. I'm changing my name to Joel Icarus Robbins. I'd love for my drone to go near the sun, but it won't leave the ground. After I received my new drone, Rod and I drove to the soccer fields again, and Rod commenced to set up and fly his drone. Nothing to it.

I, on the other hand, was going through startup steps. The manual said to connect to my phone, which acted as the video screen. Then I remembered the phone in my pocket wouldn't work with this drone, and Sara's phone, which would work, was at home. I said bye to Rod, who was too busy to respond, and drove home. Karen was doing housecleaning for me and looked up when I entered.

"Have to use the bathroom cause the ones in the park are locked"-- a bald-faced lie.

When I returned Rod was still engrossed and smiling. I started through the 6 steps again. Nothing happened. I had mistakenly picked up the manual for my former drone that had escaped a week ago and weed-whacked its way into obscurity. I told Rod I would be right back. Again, he didn't notice because he was whizzing his drone around the field, taking aerial photos and chuckling to himself.

When I reached home, I tried to enter undetected, but Karen, who was in the next room, peeked around the corner with her eyebrows raised.

"I have to use the bathroom again." Karen's eyebrows went higher. "Diarrhea," I confidently shared.

She gave me that more-information-than-I-need look. I grabbed the correct manual and drove back. Rod was there doing dives and flips--the drone, not Rod--and smirking like a schoolboy.

I started through the 6 steps, which had grown to 8. Nada. Rod's drone's batteries had run down, so he took time to read the technical manual to me through his grin. After all, he's an engineer and I'm a retired English teacher. I tried to follow: 1) switch on, 2) push the left joystick up/down, 3) push both joysticks up to the outsides, 4) turn drone horizontally counterclockwise, 5) turn it clockwise, 6) push both joysticks down to the inside, 7) take a valium, 8) push the takeoff button. Pray. Nothing.

Because I didn't want to go home without flying my drone, I picked it up and threw it as hard as I could toward the croquet field, saying, "There you go." Rod gave me a look that indicated the Valium hadn't worked, but I was finally grinning. Looking him straight in the eyes, I swore him to secrecy.

The next day's activities left me feeling like the farmer that put a box of zucchini on a chair by the road marked with a FREE sign. Returning, he found the zucchini on the ground and the chair and the sign gone. I put my new drone and my old drone's accessories on an upside-down tote in my front yard and, when I came back, the tote was gone but all the drone paraphernalia was there. I guess they had read my Facebook posts. So, I put the drone on a cardboard box with a ten-dollar bill sticking out from underneath. Uh, uh, uh, you're getting ahead of me.

With slumped shoulders and humbled head, I took the new drone inside and dumped the old drone refuse in the trash. I drone-shamed myself and took on the challenge. I put the drone on the dining room floor and puzzled through the directions. Viola, it worked and, like my wayward drone, popped up in an attempt to shear texture off my pebbled ceiling. I grabbed it just in time to avoid a plaster snowstorm.

The next day, I grabbed the correct manual, the drone and Sara's phone and drove to the soccer field. My hubris had returned. I was not an 'Icarus'; I was now a wise 'Daedalus', who was known for designing labyrinths. But not for long. I started through the steps and looked at the rear of the drone. It looked like an army transport airplane with its rear bay open and empty. I called the drone, battery, the phone and myself several unflattering names. I also sharply trimmed a nearby clump of weeds with my sneakers, then stomped up and down. I drove home to find the battery in the charger. Luckily, no one was around, but I used the bathroom just in case. Finally, back at the field, it ran perfectly and I took pictures. I sent one to Rod right away to show that I wasn't a complete drone ninny, just a partial nincompoop.

WOMEN

Women, besides higher intelligence, a caring nature and keen intuition, have better eyesight than men. Sara used to say, "Honey, look around your chair. Just look!"

I'd respond: "Okay, floor, more floor, a chair, a coffee table, more floor and over there is the focal point of my existence, the television."

"Look ON the floor."

"OK. What? Oh, the skins of Spanish peanuts?"

"Exactly! You need to control those or eat regular peanuts. They're called cocktail peanuts, Honey?"

"But I'm not having a cocktail. I'm having a Pepsi. My bifocals must have lost the bi and left only the focal. I couldn't see them."

"Why do you eat red-skinned Spanish peanuts anyway?"

Then I would explain how as a bored 14-year-old I'd ride my bicycle to the Shell station at night and hang out with the big guys sitting around the grease pit. If I had 20 cents, I could buy a 12 oz. Pepsi then walk over to the nut machine. I would gaze into its crystal ball, inside of which there was a hypnotizing and infinite supply of Spanish peanuts. You could insert 10 cents, give the knob a crank, then, magically, a handful of peanuts would cut loose, slide down a chute, knock open a metal exit flap in the base, and deliver a salty treat into my teenage hands. If I didn't have my hand ready, the turning of the crank alerted the mangy dog under a chair and it would bolt out and wolf up my peanuts from the floor before I could.

To top off this otherworldly experience, I'd drink a little of the Pepsi, then pour the peanuts down the throat of the bottle. Heavenly, a cold fizzy drink and salty goober peas all at one time. Of course, the skins floated when I drank and clung together for safety while still letting Pepsi and naked peanuts out. No, this is not going to be a rehash of an episode of Hungry, Naked and Unafraid.

The skins arrived at my throat in a wad along with the last swallow. I'd choke, cough and wheeze, but eventually the clog would cut loose and go down my drainpipe--made me sympathetic for cats hacking up furballs.

"Are you going to clean up your mess?"

Coming back to the present, I said: "Alllll right!"

"While you're at it, sweep up the bits of popcorn, Kleenex, toast crumbs, pieces of Pringles and toenail clippings."

"Next, you'll want me to vacuum the entire house."

"Okay. Thanks for offering."

I fell right into THAT trap.

Months later she greets me with: "You walked right past that dying cockroach in the hallway, Joel."

"I didn't want it! I told you the Home Defense I sprayed around the baseboards would work."

"Are you just going to leave it there?"

"Yes."

"Really?"

"Okay. Give me a Kleenex. I hate it when their tiny legs tickle my palms."

"Wuss! I picked up a big green tree frog yesterday and tossed it outside--bare handed! KLEENEX!"

She had me. I don't like picking up frogs. They feel cold and wet, like green Jello in a baggie. I especially hate it at night when I go out to take a spin in the cart and a wet amphibian—coming out of nowhere--suction-cups itself to my cheek or bare arm. Being slimed like that out of the blackness gives me the willies.

"Did you walk through Mary Carpenter's and Larry and Bonnie's yard on the way to the pool this morning?"

"Maaaybe. Why?" I respond, being careful to avoid another trap or admitting guilt if I have been reported trespassing.

"There is a trail of grass clippings running from the side door to your bedroom."

"Oh, that. I didn't see it."

"I supposed you're going to blame your bifocals on this too."

"Uh, right, good idea, I mean, yeah, my bifocals. That's the answer I was looking for."

She could see rain spots on the lanai windows while I just viewed the road, trees, birds and wall. I looked right through them, which is what I thought windows were for. Dust. It's too small and insignificant to bother with. Not Sara, she'd write "DUST ME" on my computer screen. And here I was ready to go out and buy a new monitor because the current one was beginning to fade out.

I have to look in the mirror at myself before I leave the house now, because Sara always asked at the door, "Have you looked in the mirror?"

"Yep, saw a handsome dude looking right back."

"Nope, silly, there's a grease spot and an orange glob on the belly of your shirt."

"Can't be. It wasn't there before I had a breakfast of bacon and eggs."

"You don't say!"

GLUES

I'm having trouble with the dishwasher. The cups come out with tea stains and sometimes a dish attracts a barnacle in the washing process. If it is nice and crispy, I knock it off with a flick of my finger and put it in the cabinet. I knew spinach was attracted to teeth like a magnet to a refrigerator, but I didn't know about mustard. Speaking of refrigerators, if I want to attach a doctor's appointment card to the refrigerator door, now I just squirt a smidgen of mustard on the back and whap.

When I took stage craft in college, we used casein paint--a milk product--and tempera powder to mix our own colors on the spot. I had a place in one bedroom that needed its latex paint touched up, but when I opened the old can of the correct color, all that was in the bottom was a blue sponge. The can hadn't been sealed well, and the water evaporated, leaving only a disk of porous latex. So, I found Sara's box of powdered tempera and a jug of milk and mixed up a half pint of paint. When I applied it, it matched perfectly, then it commenced to creep down the wall like a caterpillar. It didn't reach the floor, though, because Kitty Blue licked it dry first. She lived up to her name with a blue tongue for two days.

Eggs seem to love to stick to forks. That reminded me that Rembrandt painted with egg tempera, so I beat two eggs with a fork that had been washed but still had dried yolk on it. Well, why not! Then I mixed some touch-up paint with blue tempera. It came out brown. Dummy, I knew that orange and blue are complimentary colors and all complimentary colors when mixed create brown. I had worked part-time in an Ace Hardware paint department and should have known that before stirring.

So, I spooned the yolks out of two more eggs and just used the whites. Worked perfectly, but I had to keep shooing Blue, who had her tongue sticking out between her teeth, away from the wall.

I suppose I could have used flour. I often sift flour onto a dish then dip a chicken drumstick or fish fillet in it before frying. If I don't rinse the dish before putting it into the dishwasher, it comes out with a perfectly round taco shell on it. I've thought about putting several lumps of flour on a plate and just running the dishwasher's drying cycle to bake a few muffins.

Speaking of glues, I've learned that blood works well. I was a carpenter summers while teaching winters, and I was known to bleed a lot on the job. Fellow workers would yell, "Joel's on the job today; keep the tourniquets handy." So, one day I needed to glue two blocks of wood together to shim a post. Killing two birds with one stone, I cut the blocks and my index finger. I had to run to the truck to grab an oily rag to staunch the blood. When I came back, I found the blocks were already stuck together, permanently, with Robbins Brand Red Adhesive.

Elmer's glue used to be made from horses. I guess that's why the phrase 'ready for the glue factory' applied to old horses. So, I thought I'd try some hamburger as glue to stick peeling wallpaper back up. I put Blue in another room, then pinched a little meat off a patty and repaired the wallpaper. The bumps under the paper were hardly noticeable if you squinted really hard. When I opened the door again, Blue came in and sat eyeing the repair with her pink tongue licking her black lips.

I felt sorry for Blue not getting a second treat, so I dashed a dab of hamburger on the floor. As fussy cats often do, she sniffed it, but wouldn't eat. She would, though, bat it around with both paws like she was a soccer star, toss it into the air, and smear it on the floor. Luckily, I had a fresh, blue latex sponge to clean up the mess.

SHEETS

Housekeeping. Men are naturally lazy. I've learned that by being one.

I dust the floor periodically, twice a year, but, when it feels more like a beach under my bare feet than plastic laminate, I call in a professional housekeeper. I have a scoop shovel in the shed for just such occasions. Until then, I have my own gigantus sandpile to play in. Blue likes it too, but for other reasons.

Well, I washed my sheets this month. Someone questioned my only washing the sheets once a month or so. I told them that I hadn't wet the bed for a year or two. It's amazing how bringing up incontinence with someone over 70 can end a conversation in a second flat. Well, actually, it sometimes Depends on the individual.

I finally learned how to stretch on fitted sheets. My neighbor clued me in: "You follow the pattern. The stripes go lengthwise." That's it? When I get time, I'm going to ask her about 'the meaning of life, the universe and everything.'* Anyway, I tried her method and it worked.

I had always thought some bedding makers put the stripes across the bed to make it look wider, but I guess putting stripes longways makes the bed look longer. Works with shirts and dresses! What you end up choosing, I guess, hinges on whether you and your wife are fat and looking for a wide bed or tall and need a long bed. That doesn't even make sense, Joel. Now, I'm talking to myself.

With newfound knowledge, I slipped on the fitted sheet with the stripes running the length of the bed. Then I started to fill the pillowcases. Problem. The stripes went across the width of the pillow while on the bed the sheet stripes ran the length. Now I'm confused. That's the only way I could put the covers on the pillows.

Finally, I tossed the pillows up by the headboard. Lo and behold, the stripes on both the pillows and the sheet were lined up. Maybe I can figure out 'the meaning of life, the universe and everything' myself.

I had the ceiling fan turned off one day and noticed a buildup of dust and black cat fur on leading edges. Being a lax housekeeper, I decided I didn't want to get on a ladder and clean one blade at a time. Too time consuming, and I only have 16 hours of free time a day. So, I drenched all four blades with Simply Green. I picked a decorative hand towel from the linen cabinet and prepared to wipe them while standing on the floor.

When I turned the fan on high, I wasn't quick enough to get my towel in place and, like some bathtubs, I now have a ring around my bedroom. It kind of looks like a black border of something resembling fleece or velvet. I like it! The fan blades sparkle, and wiping the elegant velvet border mark from the TV, window and closet door was simple because the mixture was still moist. My friends, when they visit and see the border art, will be Simply Green with envy. Note: I did this without procuring a county remodeling permit, signing a waiver in the office, having the neighbors okay it, posting a disclaimer on my door or wearing a blue wrist band. So, don't tell anybody.

For the answer to 'the meaning of life, the universe and everything,' read The Hitchhiker's Guide to the Galaxy by Douglas Adams

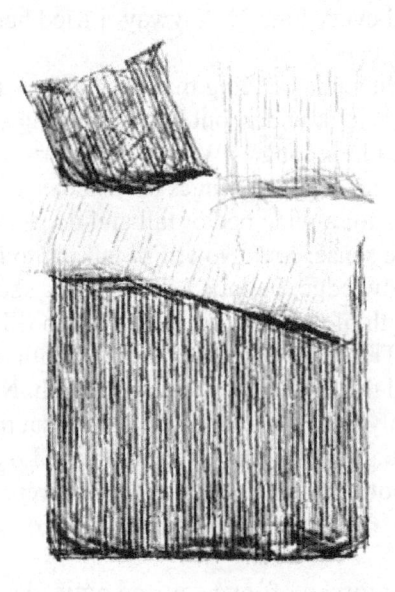

UFC

In the famous fighters' octagon, mixed martial arts proponents try to beat each others' brains out. It's called the UFC, Ultimate Fighting Championship. Well, forget the octagon and think about a square bedroom and Joel's own UFC (Unorthodox Fighting with Clothes). The things I wear always are awarded the outsized championship metal-buckled belt, while I get the macramé one I made in church camp in 1958.

The older I get the harder it is to stand on one leg to put on my boxer underwear. Twice this week, as I stumped around on the bedroom floor with one foot then the other in the air, I ended up putting each foot, one at a time, down through the right pant leg. Here I was pogo sticking it over to the wall so that I wouldn't fall down. It was like being in a one-man potato sack race. Do you know how hard it is to pull my size elevens out of one leg of boxer shorts already filled to capacity?

Of course, the other day I told about my boxers coming out of the dryer and stored in my dresser with the fly on the wrong side. If I forget and put them on that way, it is easier to go number 2 but not number 1. Last week I put my swim trunks on, locked the door, grabbed a towel, started through Mary Carpenter's yard and reached to put away my keys. There were no pockets. I looked down to see if I had put on those baggy, flame red, slick, lounging shorts Sara had bought me and said were sexy. I had been afraid to answer the door in them. No, I had on my trunks decorated with seashells and palm trees. Okay, you guessed it, I had my swimsuit on backward. Things felt a little confined, but I just put the keys into the pocket diagonally toward the back and kept going.

I've been struggling with the woven water shoes I wear to the pool. On my left foot I have a wayward little toe whose nail has whittled his way through the fabric. Every so often it decides to peek out, and I have to stop and stuff the little piggy back in.

Moving on, one day in my junior English class, a girl named Carla walked up to my desk. I knew when she had her left eyebrow raised and the right eye squinting, she was not concentrating on understanding The Pit and the Pendulum. I looked up from the papers I was grading with a wary eye.

"Mr. Robbins, stand up."

"Carla, what is it?"

"Just stand up." She had the entire class's attention, so I couldn't get out of it.

"Okay, there."

"Now step away from your desk."

The class broke out laughing.

Of course, I looked down and checked my fly first. Broken zippers are the bane of male teachers. They can expect two derailings a year. Nope, up and locked. But all the students also looked instinctively where I looked and then snapped their eyes back up, hoping they hadn't been noticed.

"What?"

"Mr. Robbins, look at your shoes." They were both wingtip style, but one was brown and one was black. The next day when I was teaching the same group of students, there was a knock on the door. I opened it and there was Jerry Johnson, the art teacher from down the hall, with a pair of shoes dangling from their shoestrings.

"Here, Joel, keep these in the bottom drawer of your desk, and you'll always have two shoes that match. They were hot pink sneakers and about two sizes too small. Then, to the delight of my students, my face turned the same color as the tennis shoes.

"Put them on, put them on, put them on!" chanted my darling wards.

UFC (Unorthodox Fight with Clothes), Episode II

When I go to the pool, I take off my ball cap, T-shirt, and water shoes. Usually, I leave my swim trunks on. It depends on who is in there already. Heck, after you're in the pool, nobody knows whether you're naked or not. I place the house keys in one shoe because I've forgotten and left them at the pool a dozen times.

While pretending to exercise, I actually gossip with other floaters and take turns at organ recitals—"My bladder started acting up yesterday," or "The doctor can't stop my left spleen from seeping," or "My toe fungus just keeps spreading." Kind of makes me want to get out of the pool. I exit with my skin looking like a dress shirt that's had rubber bands twisted on it, tie dye fashion, then hung up to dry.

Leaving the pool, I towel off, put on my T-shirt and slip my feet into my water shoes. OMG, multiple shooting pains in my left heel! Immediately I envision a trip to the podiatrist who will probably diagnose me with plantar fasci-osmosis--or something like that--a disabling heal spur or a burrowing seed wart. Then add fancy medical terminology to explain that it's most likely from a Canada thistle seed. Lifting my foot out, I'm relieved to hear my keys chiming.

Underwear always seems a problem too. It's been rumored by Sara that when I took off my shorts I did't bend over to pick them up. Instead, I looked to see if she was watching, then I did a chorus line kick with my boxers dangling from my pointing toes. The move is not worthy of being featured with the Rockettes, but my foot almost comes up to the height of my desk. The undies are supposed to flip skyward to be caught and slam dunked in the clothes hamper. Once in a while they don't come down into my hand. I find them taking a hyped-up merry-go-round ride on the fan blades. Then Sara used to wag her head from side to side and probably think, "Good heavens, I married an Emmett Kelly offspring."

I image you wives did what Sara did and bought your husband boxers with the day printed on them to keep your sweet big oaf from wearing the same pair all week, or worse, going commando. I just hate it when I grab and put on Thursday's pair on Tuesday—throws off my whole week and I walk around in a numbing fog. The only song lyrics I can remember to hum along with all day is "Here we go round the mulberry bush" instead of something like Lady Gaga's "When the sun goes down, and the band won't play, I'll always remember us this way."

KITCHEN APPLIANCES

I'm still getting used to working all the appliances. Sara always said we should remove the lower cabinets and replace them with two more dishwashers. One for dirty dishes, one for clean dishes and one partly empty. I want to save time loading and unloading the dishwasher, so instead of emptying it completely, as I remove a clean dish I replace it with a dirty dish. Well, sometimes I forget which is which, and a piece of smoked ham on a plate will taste like a two-week-old carp.

My dishes continue to come out with barnacles between the fingers of a fork or at the bottom of a cereal bowl. So, last week I added a packet of liquid soap, a squirt of Palmolive and a handful of sand. Everything came out clean, but some of the glasses are now frosted. A couple of saucers that had flowers on them now only have plant stems. One Tupperware container disappeared altogether.

The clothes washer still has too many settings, so I have Krazy glued all the setting to Presoak, Heavy, Colors (I have a racially integrated wash) and 90 Minutes. Then I Krazy glued the dryer settings to TIMED DRY--90 minutes, SIGNAL—Loud, FABRIC—Wool, and WRINKLE—I Don't Think So. After that, I pushed the Start button and about a minute later I heard the grinding of tiny gears and ran to see the Timed Dry knob eject a chunk of glue and start to move toward 0. Since I figured if it kept losing time, the clothes would never dry, I had to stand at the front of the dryer and keep twisting the knob back onto 90 Minutes.

I found our old blender and decided to make a smoothie. I looked up a recipe in veganways.com/kitchen/foods/recipes/tasteless/smoothie. I had frozen spinach, a carrot, a yam, thyme (must be a British spelling) and milk. I added a can of Pepsi for a little zip. That contributed my own personal touch to the recipe. The lid had its own lid, which seemed unnecessarily redundant. So, I just used the bigger one. I pushed the Grind button but that was too slow. Blend was better and the High button worked. When the machine reached full speed, it produced a greenish fountain from where the littlsde lid had been. I wiped down the cabinets and counter, and I poured in more Pepsi, put a plate over the hole, and continued.

About then a carrot got the best of the old Mixmaster. I left the blender on high so that it would continue as soon as I cleared the obstruction. With my left hand (don't get ahead of me, I'm telling the story) I picked up a wooden spoon and pried the carrot to the side.

The blender spun to life, but I was too slow removing the utensil. I could see many 'toothpicks' swirling around in the glass container. I stopped the blender and took out enough to refill the toothpick holder. I then pulled a now-stubby spoon out of the blender, hit the Liquify button and left it on high. The dish over the hole jumped around a bunch then settled down for the ride. The toothpicks disappeared.

I knew wood was mostly cellulite, so I googled that and found it was harmless, only causing dimples in women's bottoms. I think dimples are cute; wouldn't mind having one myself. I can't get one, though, cause I'm not a woman. I drank two glasses right off. The fizz was gone but I can recommend the drink for being mightily chewy and filling.

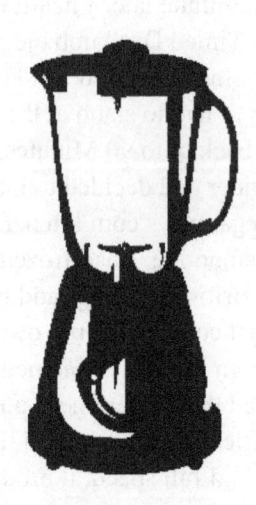

SHOES AND FEET

On the floor of my bedroom are house slippers, sneakers, black rubber mucking boots, sandals and hiking shoes. I keep dress shoes in the closet. I don't want them socializing with the riffraff. Besides, it's hard to find a place to wear them in South Florida. Well, since shoes are made for walking, that's just what they do. My slip-on sneakers often saunter under the bed, and either come out on the other side or shelter in place. I've been afraid of what's under a bed since I was a toddler.

As a grownup, I've had squirrels, bats, birds, mice, frogs, anoles, rats, tarantulas and snakes get into places I've lived or stayed. Anyway, I'm left crawling around on my hands and knees with a flashlight looking for my shoes under the bed. I'm not fond of reaching back into the dark spaces much anymore. Plus, Sara is not here to catch critters and throw them out.

Once I screamed as I reached under my bed and felt a large hairy creature. It turned out to meow just like Kitty Blue. If my espoused house slippers have a marital spat, one will hide behind my desk. I have to discipline it with the end of a yard stick. Just a couple of taps makes in come out and behave.

My gardening boots also slow me down, as if I could get any slower. Especially when I'm sprinkling Sara's garden and accidentally top off one rubber boot with water.

Either Karen, who helps me clean house, or I, while lining up my footwear against a wall, will inadvertently set a boot or right shoe on the left and the left shoe on the right. Without checking I put them on. Since I already walk like a duck and not a pigeon, having them on the wrong foot accentuates the winged image—imagine a goose instead of a duck. Some may think by the way my feet flap when I walk that I might be preparing to take flight.

When I walk down the driveway, one foot looks like it's going northeast and the other northwest, kind of like a Harley V2 engine lying on its side pumping away. Luckily they offset each other and I can proceed north. The sensation is a mite disorienting until I look through the window at my car's snow-globe-style floating compass.

I remember my little league baseball coach, Dick Hampton, watching me try to beat out an infield grounder. Viewing my attempt to hustle toward first base, he said, "That Joel can run longer in one place that anyone I've ever seen." I do entertain people walking down the street behind me, their eyes wagging side to side as if watching a two-person conversation during speed dating. With my wing like feet, I end up stubbing my two little toes on table legs, doorways and the stove at home and, on the street, recycle containers, lamp posts and pedestrians' ankles. Blue has learned to hug the wall as we pass in the hallway.

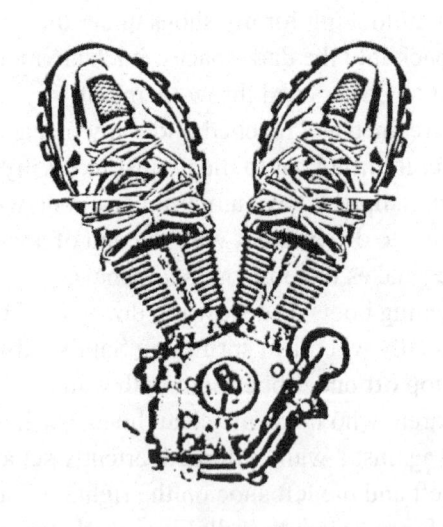

NEVER TOO OLD TO LEARN

I had an interesting day yesterday. I usually have fried eggs for breakfast, but I decided instead to have a boiled egg. I remembered that it takes three minutes for a soft-boiled egg and five minutes for a hardboiled egg. I didn't want to waste 15 minutes boiling water, cooking the egg, cooling it, and then peeling it. So I decided to use the microwave. I put the egg into a cereal bowl and filled the bowl with enough water to almost cover the egg. I used my extensive geometry skills to calculate that five minutes boiling in a pan would take about two minutes boiling in the microwave. I watched the water through 1,218 tiny holes, waiting for it to boil. Well, it sure didn't take the two minutes I thought it would. It only took 37 seconds for the egg to blow up in a spectacular way. At least the microwave received a thorough cleaning before I gave up and fried an egg.

Since this isn't my first rodeo, that was at Arcadia last summer with Rod and Lowell, I was reminded of a situation I had had when I was 8. Mom was an excellent cook. She had to be because she had her father living with us, a husband and three sons. Anyway, one day I came home from school to find a note on the kitchen table. My two other brothers were at different athletic practices, so I, an eleven-year-old, took up the message.

"There's a Dutch oven with a roast, mushrooms and carrots slow cooking. Please wash six potatoes, rub them with Crisco, place them in a rectangular Pyrex dish, turn the oven up to 375 degrees and let them cook for one hour. Then turn the oven down to 150. I should be home soon after that. P.S. Don't forget to poke each with a fork. Love, Mom." I followed her directions in chronological order. After I turned the heat down, I poked a potato and the top blew off, leaving a substantial divot.

Then I had a weighty decision to make. Was that normal or an anomaly? Should I poke the rest of them as directed or realize Mom or I had made a mistake. I chose the former and with my fork I exploded three more vegetable "grenades." I forget what Mom did to make up for the missing starch in our dinner. As for the riced potato coating sticking to the walls of the oven, luckily, Mom had a new can of Easy-Off. Twenty years later potato skins showed up on menus as an appetizer. I guess I was ahead of my time.

    I discovered something else today. For years when I would switch lanes on I-75, Sara would give the steering column the finger. The index finger. And she would wiggle it. Getting the message, I'd flip off the turn signal. How had she known it was on when I could barely see its indicator light behind the steering wheel and among all the gages? Well, today I was driving toward home and turned onto Pinebrook. All at once I heard: beep, beep, beep, beep.

    Then when I had happy hour on the porch, the cardinals and blue jays weren't just yawning every so often while they perched near the feeder. They were chirping, tweeting and peeping. Cool! Kitty Blue, who I though had a slight whistling wheeze at night, turned out to possess a distinctive snore. Not so cool. I guess my new hearing aids work.

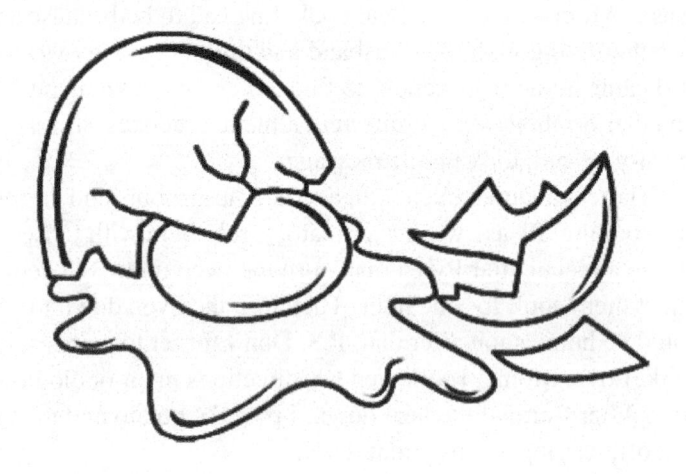

HEARING AIDS

Just at the beginning of the corona virus outbreak, Sara told me we were both going to have our hearing tested. The reasons:

We misunderstood words: For example:

Sara: "Joel, did you take out the trash?"

Me: "I'll go get some takeout food in a minute, Honey. Chinese or Mexican?"

We couldn't watch the movies we turned on; we were too distracted reading closed captions and subtitles.

We were yelling at each other outside of domestic arguments.

We hadn't retained a divorce lawyer.

The test was unsettling. Not knowing I was claustrophobic, the Audiotechnocrat told me to go into a closet with one tiny window. It looked like someone had glued egg cartons to the walls. She closed the door. I couldn't hear a thing! To make it worse she put earphones on me. I guess she wanted to show me what it's like to be completely deaf and scare me into buying the most expensive hearing devices possible.

When she turned her back, I inched the door open a little. My heart was already beating fast, my breathing rapid and my palms sweaty. Images of being bricked in as in Edgar Allan Poe's 'The Cask of Amontillado" dominated my paranoia.

The oughtologist stood up, came over and closed the door once again. She didn't blink an eye as she glared at me, which was unnerving. I adjusted my earphones, opened the door again and stuck my head out to make a request to play Broadway music. She said something I couldn't hear. I tried to read her lips. It looked like she said: "Uh toto dump ash." It didn't make any sense at all.

She came over and slammed the door. I had been told I was supposed to raise my hand if I heard anything. Summer and winter, I enjoy the buzzing sounds of cicadas in my ears, which Sara said wasn't normal. Well, it is normal for me! Since I heard noise, I put my hand up and left it up. By the squinty eyes and the pursed mouth, I determined that wasn't what the examiner wanted.

She opened the door, I lifted one earphone and she explained that I was to raise my hand only when I heard a low-pitched sound or a high-pitched sound. She said I suffered from tetanus, so I was to ignore any buzzing sounds. I was hermetically sealed up again, and I thought I detected a bolt being clanked into place. I put my earphone back over my ear while she continued pushing buttons and turning knobs. But I didn't hear anything. She was giving me a disgruntled look. I was ready to raise my hand just to show I had not suffocated in the enclosure.

Being so anxious to react, when I finally heard the first sound, my arm flew up and knocked my headphones off. She just shook her head and then flopped it down hard on the instrument panel, activating multiple buttons. Wow—Now I heard lots of sounds. Both hands and a foot were flying up and down, but she didn't notice.

Eventually, the test was over and the entomologist said the cochlear hairs in my ears had been damaged probably when I used power equipment as a summer carpenter. Did I have hair sticking out of my ears, showing split ends. Doubly embarrassing! I'd better treat my ear hair with Nexxus Repair Conditioner.

Sara was tested, and the lady told us that I had lost the high range and Sara had lost the low range. Ah ha! That's why I couldn't hear her reciting a to-do list, and she couldn't hear me say, "Not now, Honey, there's a big game on."

Months later, I went to be fitted with my new hearing aids. The optologist placed them in my ears and adjusted them. I don't know if you've ever had anyone come up behind you, put a finger in each ear, then give them a hard twist. Well, it brought me right up out of my chair. I gave her a why-did-you-do-that look and sat back down. The maneuver worked, though. The hearing aids were seated and I could hear.

Then an assistant brought out a leather jewelry case that contained a little felt purse and an engagement ring box. All were highly embossed with the hearing aid's logo. Was this a proposal of marriage? Had the fingers rotating in my ears been some kinky modern mating ritual? I grabbed the jewelry box, slid along one wall, and tiptoed sideways to exit. And ran!

CASSEROLE

For the first five and a half years of our marriage, Sara told me she didn't like different foods on her plate to touch. Most of the time she ate one item at a time until it was gone and then started on the next. She absolutely forbade me to fill a plate for her, because I'd cozy the mash potatoes up to the green beans. When ladling the gravy onto the meat, I'd flood everything on the plate. She'd almost gag when I'd dig a hole in my mashed potatoes, fill it with chicken and noodles and then garnish it with three or four spoonsful of peas. I'd stir it all together and shovel it in? She'd leave the room, choke a few times and then return.

After those first years, we had two toddlers she was chasing from room to room and picking up toys after. Then there was cleaning vomit from furniture or having to change their clothes because of accidents. Her only 'quiet' and undisturbed time during the day was when she opened the pots and pans drawer and gave each kid a wooden spoon. I came home from after-school play practice one day, and there was Sara, arms limp, shoulders drooped, lips drooped and hair kinky instead of softly curled. I smiled and asked, "What's for dinner?"

"Casserole!"

I pulled my head back and looked to see if she was serious. What happened to foods not touching? Casseroles were a virtual hug fest! She gave me that don't-you-say-a-word-buddy look. Out of the oven came a chicken and noodle dish, with tatter tots on the bottom and canned peas on top, all covered with spray-on Cheez Whiz. Now that was my kind of cooking!

Since I'm doing all the cooking, I'm experimenting. The other day I decided to prepare several of my favorite foods. I trimmed off the pithy bottoms of seven asparagus spears and placed them on a dinner plate. I slathered them with butter and topped that off with a ham steak to let their savory juices mingle. I cut a tomato in half and lay it on one side of the plate for color and ambience. On the other side I dropped a haystack of shredded cheese. I finished by adding a large slice of sweet onion. I spilled perfectly round drops of A1 sauce across the plate the way they do in high class restaurants to add ten dollars to an entrée. It was a gourmet dish to behold. Then I popped the plate into the microwave.

It was a fancy TV Dinner without the dividers. You'd have been surprised. I had taken four delicious foods and removed all the taste. The tomato was the only item that was truly edible, and it was mushy. The asparagus spears were crunchy, the ham watery, the onion smelly and the cheese lumpy. Mushy, Crunchy, Watery, Smelly and Lumpy. Weren't those the names of the Seven Dwarfs' five cousins?

Since becoming tired of the same old diet sodas, I've regressed to the days when I sat on a revolving red stool at a soda shop counter and ordered a cherry, lemon or vanilla coke. I still make those, but I've moved up in the world of fruity tastes. I buy peach or black cherry Fresca and then add fresh strawberries or frozen blueberries. Pushing a potato masher to the bottom of the glass releases the fruit flavor. Just don't push too hard or you'll receive a zesty facial with a blueberry up your nose, as I did.

BEING ADAPTABLE

Sara always had me buy Handi Wipes, but I nicknamed them Hardli Wipes. I've now thrown them all away. Why? With my fingers spread, from the tip of my little finger to the tip of my thumb it's more than nine inches. When I'd grab a Hardli Wipe to clean a dish or counter, it balled up to the size of a cotton ball. It's like cleaning the toilet with a Q-tip.

It took forever with that one square inch of material to cover just the acreage from the refrigerator to the sink, let alone on to the end of the counter or the entire center island. If a bump in the road like a dollop of dried catchup wouldn't let loose, I'd squish up my face and apply as much elbow grease as I could muster without success. Now I use a hot pad mitten as a dish cloth.

How do you know when it's time to toss the dish cloth into the washer? If you find yourself opening the kitchen waste basket several times to take a smell. Or covering your nose with a hanky while shining a flashlight into the garbage disposal. Or exhaling into your hand then sniffing the trapped air. It might be the dishcloth.

Do you know you can use the sink sprayer to wash the windows above the sink? It saves a bunch of time and Windex. And there are always embroidered napkins handy to wipe them dry.

I had to be extremely adaptable today, The Fourth of July. Our club hosted an ice cream social. Although I was being faithful to my keto diet, I knew I couldn't social distance from a bowl of ice cream topped with hot fudge and peanuts. So, at the appointed hour for the party, I pulled my chair up to the open freezer door, pulled out ice cubes one at a time, dipped them in nonfat powered milk and licked it off. The sink full of diminished cubes looked like an Alaska ice flow had broken up.

Because of trying to not be a covid-19 statistic, I've learned to play cards with a make-believe opponent, Albert. We tried playing gin rummy the other night, but I became too tired to finish the game. Well, I had to draw a card or play and discard, get up and walk around the table, play, draw, or discard, get up and walk around the table... I was ahead of Al, though, when we quit. I'm really good at winning at Hearts, too. When I play euchre, I get dizzy circling the table. The four make-believe-player card games with Albert, Mobly, Delbert and myself make my schizophrenia act up.

SCAVENGER HUNT

The first non-annual Fifth of July KGC Golf Cart Scavenger Hunt is over. I organized the hunt because Sara and I had thoroughly enjoyed the one during KGC Games this year. Plus, those who were left behind in Florida by the snowbirds—thank you very much, fair-weather friends--are bored out of their gourd. More than a week ago, Ron Peltier drove me around the club, and I hopped out to shoot 15 pictures and note the associated addresses. I whittled the number down to 12 for the event.

About 16 carts--give or take a couple of drive-bys that slowed, rubbernecked and drove on--clustered in the lot outside the Art/Craft Room. It was obvious most of the participants had never been in the military or a parochial school, because the drivers could not muster their carts into any recognizable or standard formation.

Since the vehicles were staggered or one in front of another or sideways or under a tree in the shade, I was afraid to drop the green flag. I called out that I didn't want the first five minutes to be a carnival bumper-cars event. They weren't listening.

I was worried because, just as you never put your finger on a pistol trigger until you've stopped waving it around and are pointing at your target, you don't put your foot on the accelerator until you've straightened your wheels and you're ready to rock and roll.

I had given them a sheet of 12 photos of objects they had do find inside the KGC environs. They had to write the house numbers below them. I counted down and they lurched forward, narrowly missing each other and grinning like a toddler eating his first Gummy Bear.

Luckily, there were no scrapes or T-boning. That may have been because while they were lining up, I told them a cautionary tale: Tom McIntosh had been T-boned at the corner of 41 and Laurel that morning. He was bumped and bruised, and the car was totaled.

Being the well-organized person that I am, once they left, I set up the table so that I could check their papers when they returned.

Gosh dang &@#%X! I couldn't locate the answer sheet. #&@#%! Luckily, no one was in the room that I was turning blue.

Then I wondered if I had given it to participants in one cart by error. %$&#@. Now the room was a deep shade of blue. The answer sheet looked exactly like the others. I had no way of knowing if someone was driving around thinking, "This is easier than I thought." Or "Is Joel playing a devious trick?" Or "What do we do when we drive to the house number listed on the paper, just circle the picture and Joel's answer as if that proves we were there?"

I jumped into my cart and raced home, taking back streets so the participants would not discover my faux pas. Just like my keys, phone and wallet when I lose them, the answer sheet was right where I had left it. Breathing less frantically, on the way back several participants caught me out.

I received offers of bribes for answers, I saw a driver take her hands off the wheel and throw them into the air in frustration, and one yelled that they needed two more hours. Others made verbal comments that I'm probably glad I couldn't make out.

Sue Green and Jim Mosher came in first, Debbie and Gordon Hatch, second, and Barb and Rocky Knuth, third. Patti Murphy and Josi Merkin were a close fourth. You always must have participation awards or people sulk, even old people. So, since I didn't have ribbons, each person was presented with a silver medal, well, at least a silvery wrapped Klondike bar. Several forgot they were wearing virus protection and painted square, chocolate brown lips on their masks.

HARRY POTTER'S KITCHEN

Navigating the kitchen is like trying to follow the plot of a Harry Potter book. Almost every morning I fry two eggs for breakfast. After that I have to use steel wool to remove bits of egg from the cast iron skillet. Sara could fry an egg, slide it in circles around the bottom of the pan and slip it onto a plate with the panache of a sous-chef. What am I doing wrong? I mentioned my problem to a neighbor lady.

"Never ever wash a cast iron skillet!" she scolded me.

"Sorry," I apologized, hoping her feeling weren't hurt, then we went on to other subjects,

So, I didn't! But a crust of a quarter inch built up on the skillet in only one week. Out of that poked half-inch spikes of charred egg, cheese, hamburger bits and onions. They grabbed the eggs and didn't let them slide out of the frying pan. My favored once-over-lightly eggs always turned out scrambled. Back to my neighbor lady. I told her about the crusty pans.

"Ok. How many cast iron pots and pans do you have?"

"Three skillets and a Dutch oven."

"Wash them and scrape all the food out. Then season them overnight."

"Okay," I responded, even though I was sure she had told me to "never, ever, no never, da, da de dumb," but then we went on to other subjects.

Hence, I took out the three sizes of skillets and the Dutch oven, washed each, placed them on the counter and seasoned them. The small one I use for eggs, so I salted it with salt and peppered it with pepper. The middle sized one Sara used for oriental dishes, so I sprinkled it with curry powder, cumin, coriander, star anise, a dash of turmeric then a pinch of saffron for color (read about the color trick online). I had to google oriental spices, and, amazingly, those were all in Sara's spice rack.

Then I turned to the Dutch oven. Sara would brown a roast, season it, add mushrooms, potatoes, onions, carrots and water, cover it with a cast iron lid and let it bake for hours. Therefore, after googling again (I like googling and being googled, don't you?), I seasoned it with bay leaves, garlic powder, onion powder and dried parsley. The large frypan she used for preparing taco meat. That was strewn by me with chili powder, paprika, oregano and black pepper.

I left the pans on the counter overnight as directed, shook out the spices in the morning, sneezed three times--causing Kitty Blue to execute a backflip and disappear under the sofa--and put the two large ones and the Dutch oven away. I sprayed some Pam into the small skillet and fried my eggs with a dusting of Parmesan cheese on top. Well, I'm beginning to distrust the neighbor lady. There were patches of crisp egg and carbonized cheese sticking to the bottom and sides of the skillet.

The next day I saw my neighbor lady at her mailbox. She asked about my children and grandchildren and then my frying pans. I told her my story. She gave me that "poor clueless males" look and explained that seasoning pans means oiling them then leaving them in a warm oven overnight. How was I to know that? When Sara was fixing a Thanksgiving dinner and needed help, she'd tell me to season something, such as cooked carrots, and put them on the table. That meant butter, salt and a drizzle of honey. There was no overnight in the oven about it!

I thought that cast iron pots and pans were fifty shades of gray, but, now that I have them 'seasoned,' I see they're black. "The pot calling the kettle black" proverb finally makes sense.

KITCHEN TOOLS

I think Sara had more tools in the kitchen than I do in the shop. She didn't recognize many of mine and, guess what, I can't identify many of hers.

There's specimen 1. It's too small and delicate to squeeze lemons, so maybe it's for juicing a strawberry. Who squeezes strawberries? But if someone does juice strawberries, who would squeeze them one at a time! Maybe it makes meatballs. Or captures a fly in the soup--dead or alive. If it were in Sara's chest of drawers with the fancy ribbons and fine net pouches, I'd guess it's a potpourri packer—a sachet for someone that likes to sashay around.

Number 2. It's real tin, which means it's older than I am but less tarnished. Looks like something you might cover a soda pop can with, but there's a hole in the middle that would let the honeybees and sugar wasps in. A branding iron for moon pies?

Then there's Number 3. It's a dome with a handle and a screw-on lid. The lid has tiny holes in it. I think it's a cover for a fried egg on a plate to keep it hot while letting the steam out. Probably of British origin. Better yet, it might cover an egg cup. Just screw off the lid and there's your egg, pointy end up.

The fourth one is obviously a mallet or hammer. I could use something like that in my shop when I want to distress a piece of furniture to make it look shabby chic. Maybe it's used to put texture in plaster when a hole is being patched in the ceiling. No, it's in the kitchen! I may repurpose it to curry Kitty Blue. Now I use this 100-wire curry brush that looks like it could scrape paint off a bulldozer.

That brings me to a jar filled with baby shower-caps. My mom wore a larger clear cap when it rained or snowed to protect her permanent. I guess it wasn't a permanent or she wouldn't have had to protect it. Anyway, these are even smaller than the little ones placed in hotel bathrooms. With them adorning jars on the counter and in the refrigerator, it's like having elves wearing plastic berets keeping me company. When I open the door to the refrigerator I say: "Hello there! Welcome, tiny fellows."

I'd seen Sara use a peach-colored one to cover a small bowl of peaches she couldn't finish. So, I guess they're color coded. I use a green one to over my rice jar because rice is a green plant. Purple was as close to brown I could come for an open can of root beer. Yellow works well for a half of a golden delicious apple, as you can see, but also to cover an onion half, staying fresh in a saucer of water. Of course, you can see through them, but I like the color coding anyway.

Just to prove I'm not a dummy, I did figure out one weird kitchen tool of Sara's. It has concentric stainless-steel rings, a web of wire making a sieve affair and a handle. I googled it and found its names: spider strainer, fry colander or skimmer. I use it in the litter box, which I find more rewarding than hooking and netting fish, because on each dip I land a big one.

GOLFING

I haven't been golfing for 40 years, except for miniature and ladder golf, so I went to a sporting goods store and bought a Dynamics driver, putter and one named Burst. Since a driver is for distance and a putter for close in, I assumed the Burst is for in between.

As I was leaving the shop I remembered a quotation by the famous journalist H. L. Menchen: "If I had my way no man guilty of golf would be eligible to any office of trust or profit under the United States." I thought about present and past presidents back to Truman.

I decided to play nine this morning at the Pinebrook Park Course to test out the new purchases. It was 91 degrees with 73% humidity, but I walked it anyway.

When I approached the first tee, I grabbed my driver and looked for the green. Nothing. Woods on both sides. A couple that was also playing could tell I was a newb. They pointed and said something about a dog's leg to the right.

"What?"

"There's a dog leg to the right."

I guess I heard them correctly. I walked forward a little, hoping to scout out the dog's leg, which I assumed was detached and several days old. I absolutely wanted to avoid it, but I didn't see or smell a thing.

Going a little farther I finally saw the flag. I went back to the tee and fired away. I heard the lady tell her husband, "Hook." I looked around again, expecting to see the dog's leg hanging from a tree by a hook. Still, I didn't see it. I began to wonder what kind of weird course this was.

Every time a fly buzzed around my head or landed on my lips or nose, you know what I was thinking—that rotting leg has to be near me somewhere.

On the second shot, I could see the flag easily, and when I cut loose, the man said, "Slice." I wished he and his wife would quit talking about that severed canine appendage. It was giving me the willies.

On the next tee, I let loose again. The helpful man behind me told me to twist my body more to gain distance. Two more shots and I was in. The lady then said something about a "birdie." Finally, something besides that poor three-legged pup. I said: "Thanks, I'll look for it. I could hear the birdie, a cardinal, I think, but I couldn't see it.

I continued to play and sweat, and the couple followed me. I was ready to let them play through, but they were giving me warnings and pointing out wildlife. Friendly folk. I approached the next tee and the man yelled, "Dog leg left." Now the poor pooch was down to two good legs.

On the next shot I bounced one off a tree and it went into the bushes.

"Rough" was the only word of a sentence I heard from the lady.

"It sure is!" I responded, but I didn't care how tough it was to play the course, I kept going.

Walking to the next tee, a three-foot snake slithered across my path. I did a little high-stepping, yelped and threw my driver at him. Missed. "Just another Florida golf hazard," laughed the man.

I finished the course drenched in sweat. The couple finished and strolled over.

"What did you shoot?" he asked.

"37."

"I shot 31 and my wife shot 29. What's your handicap?"

I didn't realize that I had played that badly. I tried to make some excuses: "I'm not handicapped. I'm very old and mightily awkward."

With that I picked up my equipment and drove home. Despite the unusual events during my outing, I concluded that I liked Frisbee golf.

TROUBLESOME KITTY BLUE

Black kitty hair is taking over the house. I brush Blue with a torturous instrument that porcupines out 132 springy wires. The one I use is labeled a "pet pin slicker brush." Blue seems in love with it. So, I have the grooming tool in one hand--brushing and collecting hair--and a tissue in the other to wipe the drool from her smiling lips. If I don't, there are wet spots on the light blue, yellow, orange and green cover of my foot stool where she sits.

The multi-pin slicker brush works well, except when I remove the hair trapped in the needle-like wires. I inevitably run one pin far up under a fingernail. Then my left leg flies up as if a doctor has hammered my kneecap with the round head of a ballpeen hammer. Blue lands several feet away, looks over her shoulder at me and wonders why I dropkicked her across the room. I love her up with an adolescent boy's soprano "nice kitty, pretty kitty, kitty, kitty, kitty...." She glides behind her climbing tower without taking her eyes off me.

Sara always had what was advertised as the "best pet hair remover in the world." It's a roller with a sticky surface that when peeled off has another sticky surface under it. She would roll it over the seat cushions of the lanai chairs before company arrived. I found it and removed an old tacky layer that looked like a black angora rag.

I decided to not treat the symptoms but the cause. So, I rolled it along Blue's back to take care of the problem at the source. Blue took exception to the treatment and gave the roller a nip. But it worked! The sticky paper was covered with black hair, and Blue came through it with only one injury—a patch of snowy white bare skin on her left hip. A short spray of Krylon matte black camouflaged that.

When Karen comes to the house and dry mops under and behind the furniture, she ends up with a pile of debris that looks like dried fish food with fishing bobbers in it. The "fish food" is probably catnip and the bobbers are Blue's ping pong balls. Oh, and with black cat hair hovering in the air above the pile.

Besides being hairy, Blue exhibits other traits that annoy me. Her nightly ritual takes place after I have read myself cross-eyed in bed, tossed away the second pillow, turned out the light and rolled over on my side. Aaaaah! Then the cat performs a solo stampede from the lanai, through the living room, through the dining room, through the kitchen, down the hallway and across Sara's bedroom floor. You'd swear she had eight to ten paws.

It reminds me of my children when they were young. They almost always became hyper when it was getting close to bedtime. If Blue's extremely antsy, she runs the "raceway" in reverse. If she doesn't, I lie there wide-eyed waiting not for the proverbial other shoe to drop, but the "other paw."

FIRE

    Neighbor: "What's new?"
Me: "I had a fire at my house last night."
"Oh. Sorry to hear that."
"No. I started it myself."
"Really! You have a more serious problem than I thought."
"No. It was in my fire pit behind my house."
"Whew! I'm relieved. You had me worried for a second."

    It had rained much of the day and the temperature had cooled. I usually only start a fire in the winter, but I wanted to clean up some of the wood stacked behind my house, plus I didn't know how I was going to occupy my evening. Sitting in front of a fire produces unusual effects, pleasant and unpleasant.

    As soon as the fire was blazing nicely, I had to go to the bathroom. What is it about a fire that makes boys and men want to get a hose out and spray something? Is it the childhood admiration of firemen? It happens every time for me. I might as well light a match standing over the toilet and have done with it. Having this condition used to make Sara laugh. With her the stimulus to relieve herself was getting into a car to travel a long distance. She'd have me stop so she could potty at every rest stop on the way.

    Mom and Dad hadn't talked to me about this phenomenon. I knew about the running water trick, though. I'll never forget having to produce my first specimen at about nine. The nurse handed me an orange-juice glass and told me she needed a sample. She hustled me into the restroom and closed the door. I opened it a little, peeked out, and Mom was there, knowing I needed an explanation.

    "Pee in the glass, honey."
"Why would I do that?"
"Just do it, please."
"Will I get spanked? Like the time Jon had me tell Dad at breakfast: 'Here's a glass of apple cider.'"

    Mom covered a giggle with her hand and said, "No. The nurse needs to use your pee for a test."

    "Why? Is she going to play a trick on the doctor?"

She pushed me back into the bathroom and closed the door.

Five minute later I stepped out with an empty glass.

"I can't." I was almost in tears.

"Yes, you can. I'll come in with you."

Well, that was a mistake. It's lefty loosie and righty tighty when it comes to faucets. Having Mom watching over my shoulder was turning my faucet handle mighty tighty. She realized her mistake and said:

"Ok. Listen, when I leave, turn on the faucet and let it run."

"Why? Do you want me to fill the glass and pretend it's pee?"

"No, sweety. It'll make you want to go."

"I want to go now, Mommy. Home!"

Well, as we all know, the running water magic works. Even today, when I'm rinsing the dishes, I have to stop and go to the bathroom. And when I am washing the car. And when I am listening to the washing machine fill up.

Finally successful, I opened the door slowing and carefully, balancing the juice glass so it wouldn't spill. Only the laws of surface tension were helping me avoid disaster. As when Dad used to tell the gas station attendant: "filler up," I filled her up and topped her off. I was beaming and shuffling forward, but Mom and the nurse were inching backward; neither wanted to touch my proud liquid accomplishment.

MORE GETTING FIRED UP

Sara and I let our neighbors know that if they saw us around the fire pit, they were welcome to join us. We oldies in Florida say we like the beach and being outside, but that's a myth. We say we like to hike in a park, but don't, and we say we love the sun, but spend most of our time hugging an A/C unit. Kind of like we cozied up to a heater in the winter up north and stayed inside to avoid falling down on the ice, sliding are vehicle into a snowy ditch or careening sideways through a bridge whose "surface freezes before the roadway."

In Florida, it's 10 seconds outside from the house to the car parked in the carport, one minute from the car to the grocery store or restaurant, one minute back to the inside of the car, 10 seconds from the car to the house, two minutes to the mailbox and back inside the house. If we don't walk the streets or ride a bicycle, it's 23 hours and 47 minutes a day inside the house and all the rest of the time avoiding the atmosphere we moved to Florida for.

I love some of the conversations we've had when we've invited a couple to enjoy the fire.

"Sara and I are going to have a bonfire Saturday night. If you'd like to come, bring a chair and your favorite drink."

"Is it going to be outside?"

"I hope so" is what I want to say, but I quell my sarcastic spirit and say, "Yes."

"In your yard?"

"On the lanai" is what I want to say, but I exercise quelling again and say, "Yep."

"Out on the grass or is there a concrete patio?"

"Just grass."

"How long will we have to be outside?"

"A couple of hours, but you won't be required to stay outside any longer that you want to."

"Well, I don't know. You're sure it's outside."

"I'm sure."

When they come it's also an entertaining experience?

Neighbor lady: "There's sparks."
Me: "Yes."
"Lots of them. They're coming at me."
She pulled a can of Raid out of her purse and sprayed a particularly menacing spark to extinguish it. That lit things up for an instant—flamethrower in a can.

Who gets to be master in arms of the poker? Sara would wrestle it from me—ME, the mighty keeper of the fire--and hand it graciously to a guest. Sacrilege!

Once she handed it to a wife, who tried to hand it to her husband, but he was looking the other way.

"Do you want to play with the poker?" she asked him.

I think, did she say, "PLAY with the poker!" That's demeaning the power inherent in Merlin's magic wand of fire, Prometheus's scepter, Hecate's dual torches, Zeus's lightning bolt, the flaming torch carried by Mercury.

The husband answers, "Sure, I'll play poker. Straight or Texas Hold'em?"

"You didn't wear your hearing aids again, did you? Here's the poker, a POKER. Take the poker."

"Poke her? Poke who? What'd she call you?"

Without thinking, she slapped it into his hand, and, to this day, he has an L-shaped brand on his palm.

"When we've had a fire, we'd sometimes have people bring musical instruments: Tom, a clarinet; Sheldon a mandolin; David a guitar; and so on. Sometimes they'd sing, sometimes we'd all sing along and sometimes they'd tell me to stop singing. I'm the only person I know that was invited to remove himself from a church choir.

Fire and its cohort, smoke, have a conspiratorial streak. Wisps from burning embers curl up nicely as those around the fire pit warm their hands, sip their wine, stare dreamily into the flames and softly reminisce. Then arrives a nonsmoker who hates the smell of wood burning. The fire dances with anticipation and a trail of smoke creeps along the ground and swirls up the entire length of the newcomer, enveloping his head. If he moves, the smoke follows him like a compass needle to iron, like a wasp to an open can of Fanta orange soda, like flies to chicken soup, like bird droppings to your sparkling windshield.

Geriatric musical chairs ensues—"take mine," "sit here," "try this one," "it not smoky here"—it's up down, up down, until the teary-eyed, coughing sufferer gives up and moves out of the orchestra pit to the cheap seats in the second circle of chairs.

LAKESIDE WRESTLING

The other day I was invited to kayak. I mistakenly said Okay. I was reminded of spending time at Sara and my lake cottage in northern Indiana. One year, I told her I was going to buy a kayak.

She said, "Buy two."

"Why two?" I asked, "You won't go."

"Yes, I will."

"No, you won't"

"BUY TWO."

I bought two and Sara went once, I think.

She enjoyed the kayaks immensely, though. Whenever I would drag my blue and white kayak down the hill to the water, she would stop whatever she was doing. If the grandkids where visiting, she'd command them to put down their video games and come to the picture window.

"Grandpa is going kayaking!"

"So?" They would say in unison then back to gaming.

"Put them down NOW, or there will be no mac and cheese for lunch and no popsicles for the afternoon snack. Instead we'll have liver and onions and stale crackers and water.

"Ooooookay." With blank faces they would stroll over to the window with passive-aggressive slowness. My dog Tina was already there looking and whining because she wasn't with me.

"Watch this," Sara would suggest through a girlish giggle.

On one such occasion, as I turned around to pick up the paddle, the kayak sailed out to sea with me left on the pier. A few attempts to hook it with the paddle made me lose my balance, and I almost went in. Inside the grandkids were now interested, seeing me teetering on one foot, paddle outstretched and whacking at the water in one direction, while the other bare foot was bobbing high in the air behind as a counterweight.

"Hey, I learned a move like that in ballet," commented my granddaughter.

I gave up and walked into the lake and retrieved the kayak. I raised one leg to knee height and put it into the boat. Then I gave a jump to land my butt onto the seat. The far edge of the kayak flipped and punched me in the left kidney. Then the entire boat pinned me under water.

…

I had flashbacks to having a similar experience when trying to climb into a hammock for a relaxing snooze. When I had hoisted my derriere into the hammock, the hammock twisted me judo-like and threw me to the ground, knocking the wind out of me and spraining a shoulder. From my prone viewpoint on the grass, I studied the hammock label attached to the underside to see if it was made by the New England Kayak Works.

…

"Where'd G-pa go?"

"Oh, he'll come up. He's under the kayak sniffing the fishy smell trapped in the air pocket. Can't you hear him yelling?"

"Mom and dad won't let us say those words."

I lifted the kayak over my head to empty the water. First there was a mighty sucking sound as the kayak broke the surface. With me as the human fulcrum the boat seesawed back and forth as the water sloshed from end to end. I heard noises and saw three silhouettes waving delightedly behind the cottage window.

Climbing back onto the pier, I decided to try a dry boarding. With one foot in the kayak and the other on the pier, I experienced the kayak leaving port on its own again, then—just before another dunking—I heard my granddaughter yell, "G-pa is better at doing the splits at 70 than I am at ten."

I thought my swim trunks would rip, but I lurched over into the water before that happened. Back to a wet boarding I went. I jumped into the kayak fanny first and got stuck—head and shoulders sticking out on one side and my calves and feet the other. The paddle was on the pier and the kayak embarked a third time. My arms and legs were flailing but not reaching the water for locomotion. I had to rock back and forth until I was upside down under the water. Bent over with my head between my knees I crab walked my way out of the water with the kayak still attached to my rump.

"Cool!" my grandson yelled while jumping up and down.

After reorganizing, I finally entered the kayak safely and was paddling out. Then my grandson let Tina loose. She reached the end of the long pier just as I was paddling alongside. At full gallop she dived for the open cockpit. You can image the chaos of splashing arms, legs and paws as the kayak floated lazily away empty.

KAYAK Continued

You know about how much fun Sara had watching me enter and exit a kayak. The story really begins when Sara brought home a beautiful canoe that her father had found in Carmel, Indiana. We had only been married two years, so sharing a small apartment was still a daily ego test. We were marking our territories like siblings slapping each other's hands and kicking each other's feet when they intruded into the invisible DMZ down the middle of the back seat of their parents' car. Who would captain the canoe?

There's a progression of canoe materials aimed at reducing weight: Aluminum, polypropylene, Kevlar and carbon fiber were the lightest. The one Sara bought was an over-engineered, one-of-a-kind prototype--thick, reinforced, heavy fiberglass. I think I popped my first hernia lifting it off the station wagon roof rack.

We didn't have any money to stay in motels or cruise the rivers and lakes in a ski boat, so we camped in a pup tent and recreated on rivers in our canoe. The first time out, I sat in the back and Sara sat in the front. She tried to steer from the front while I tried to steer from the back. Therefore, we plowed sideways in the river most of the time.

Sara, "Why are we standing still?"

Me: "Just paddle, dear. The person in the back is the one that steers."

"But you were going to hit that rock."

"No, I was slowing turning away from it. Then you…"

"Hey, buddy boy, I'm in the front. You were going to hit the rock."

"Because you want to steer, my hat is now back there hooked to a branch."

"If we had hit that rock, you would have thrown me out," Sara countered.

"If you keep steering, that might be a good idea" I mumbled to myself.

"What?"

"Nothing, dear."

"I just had my hair straightened, you don't want to get it wet and go all frizzy, do you?"

"Heaven forbid!"

I wanted to add: "Why do you think they put rudders in the rear of water craft, Dear," but I didn't want to sleep outside the tent that night while being crawled on, pawed, and picked over by the inevitable family of marauding racoons, then pin-pricked by several swarms of vampirish mosquitoes.

After a weekend camping and canoeing, I had several good ideas:

1) Sell the canoe in order to save the children we were planning to start producing in a year.

2) Ministers, instead of counseling a couple about marriage before the wedding, should loan them a pup tent and a canoe and send them on a weekend outing. If they still wanted to get hitched after that, let them have a go at it. Biblical parables don't hold a candle to first-hand chaos.

3) When a divorce lawyer's business gets slow, advertise free use of canoes for married couples only. The lawyer's phone number and logo would be displayed prominently on the outside of the canoes.

One time, my buddies and I traveled to Minnesota's Boundary Waters to canoe and fish for a week. The canoeing from island to island was fine, but the portages of a half mile or so were brutal. I ended hauling a 60 lb. Grumman aluminum canoe on my shoulders and a 70 lb. waterproof pack on my back. That's where I popped hernia number 2.

My first canoe partner on the trip, like my wife, wanted to guide from the front, so when the other canoes traveled 7 miles in a straight line, we traveled 11 in a zig zag pattern. The next time we were teamed up, I jumped into the front seat of the canoe before he could so I would be the locomotion and he the rudder-man.

I wish I had known about kayaks.

Speaking of kayaks, it was by accident I found out about them. I was having breakfast with my buddies one morning at a donut shop. We all claimed to be outdoors men, but mostly we watched the Adventure Channel while cuddling a can of Pringles and a six pack of Bud, practically prone on a La-Z-Boy.

The donut shop was known for its elephantine caramel glazed cinnamon rolls that were a cause of the local outbreak of Type 2 Diabetes. Two of the guys had the rolls, I had an apple fritter, and one had a Danish. Then while switching back and forth between discussing the relative merits of different pastries and rugged sports, someone mentioned something about "a kayak Eskimo roll." That sounded delicious to me because I really loved Eskimo pies.

Sara and I bought two kayaks up north and another two here in Nokomis, Florida. I know what an Eskimo roll is now, but I have never attempted one. Probably because I wouldn't be able to turn the kayak upright again. That would force me to paddle the kayak upside down, inverted submarine style, with its hull showing like the back of a manatee.

So, instead of the Eskimo roll, after sliding onto the ramp, I execute the Nokomis Flop. I extract my legs, then plop my body out of the kayak onto my back, feet in the air, roll over on my belly, pull my knees up under me and stand. It's a full body workout.

25

KGC WATER EXERCISES

When we first moved to King's Gate Club, Sara decided to participate in the water exercises Mondays, Wednesdays and Fridays for 35 minutes each time. I was playing tennis three times a week for about an hour each time—that was enough exercise for me.

One morning when I wasn't playing Tennis, Sara asked, "Why don't you come to water exercises with me?"

"What's it like?"

"Just a set of movements that work every muscle and joint."

"Who's there?"

"Barb, Mary, Jean, Bonnie, Bev, Carol, Lynn, and a few others."

"It's a women's group."

"NO IT IS NOT. You'd like it."

Well, after back and double knee surgeries, my tennis days were over. I went several times with Sara. Eleven women and Joel. Or eight women and Joel. Nine women and Joel.

"What do you think?"

"It's for women."

"NO IT IS NOT."

I started to explain that a men's exercise group would not have a woman's sweet, soothing voice giving directions with Neil Diamond crooning in the background. The narrator would have the smoker's bass voice of an Army drill sergeant. There would be periodic swearing. There would be "We Are the Champions" playing in the background.

"You're just being silly, macho man."

Then I told her to think about the names of the exercises. If you expect men to participate, when jogging in place and pumping your arms in unison, never say "make your arms move like a choo choo train." There are no choo choos in a male workout.

"That's just one exercise."

So, I went on to the "flamingo," where we're asked to stand on one leg with the other leg bent so that its foot touches the side of the knee--"and a one and a two and a one and a two and...." Call it "the Eagle," maybe, with directions: "tear the eyes out of that snook, loser. Or rip its fins off. Come on, pull its guts out. A one and a two and a one...."

Then there's one that has us hug ourselves. There's never been hugging anywhere in a man's exercise routine.

The "pendulum" directs us to swing one leg forward and backward, forward and backward. If this were a male workout, it would be called the "wrecking ball." "Knock down the building, wuss," or "kick that football through the uprights. Put your leg into it, weakling. One kick and a two and a one and a two...."

The "Mae West" would be named the "Rambo," "Dirty Harry" or "Terminator." An exercise with the arms bent and the elbows together would not come with the directions to "move your arms back and forth like a washing machine." The routine requiring the exerciser to open and close the legs would be named something other than "scissors." How about "pruning shears" or "bolt cutters."

"Pedal the bicycle" would be called "Start your Harley," vintage style. Instead of pedaling, the exerciser would kick the starter lever with one foot then the other. It's more manly! Then there's "pull the rope." Noooo! Make it "tug of war" or "snap the locker-room towel against someone's behind."

"Okay, Okay. You're right," admitted Sara. "That's enough."

But I was on a roll. One routine name surprised me, but I understood immediately--"fire hydrant." We were told to lift one leg, bend it at the knee and then straighten it out. My childhood dog Spot used to do that all the time, I told Sara.

I like going to water exercises now, I love the women there, and they enjoy teasing me. I don't look behind me anymore to see if a man is watching me performing a ballet move where my one hand and arm gracefully curve over my head and my other hand's fingertips touch my opposite shoulder. I even set a record this week and attended all three days in one week for the first time. Well, the exercise girls may give me a ribbing, but with this I am getting back at them a little.

ONLINE DATING

I accidently signed up for online dating. Mistake! It's too soon after Sara's passing to date, but I want to eventually, especially after 59 years of loving female companionship. I had heard lots of people use internet dating services. In preparation for that future day, I read about them, but that didn't help much. They all bragged about people meeting the love of their life then walking the beach at sunset each night for the rest of their lives. I figured I'd have to pick a site, sign up, pay a bunch of money to see how they actually worked. That's where the accident happened.

The one I picked sounded innocuous enough—Elite Singles. Now that rings of snobbery, but it was a site for old, wrinkly, grouchy and cranky people, most with some post high school education. Since they didn't want to call it OLD GROUCHY GRADS, they used the euphemism Elite Singles. Actually, it's a good site.

Every day I receive photos of 20 to 30 women, supposedly fitting the parameters I chose (67 to 75 and within a 50-mile radius). Also, there is a long list of answers about what type of guy they're looking for. Things like humorous, loving, a good listener, Christian, nonsmoker, hates fishing and hunting, social drinker is fine, college degree, likes shopping, free spirit, honest, is kind to small animals, etc.

Despite the parameters, I get notices from people in Miami, Detroit, Michigan, Tallahassee, Jacksonville, etc. and girls in their 50's and women in their 8o's. So, each day I look through the pictures and give them the "would I kiss this woman" scrutiny. There is an **X** and a ☺ next to the photos, which means I can delete them or send them an emoji. So I sit there thinking, I won't kiss that one, X, too far away, X, looks like my Aunt Squatty, X, too short, X, taller than I am, X, too old, X, too sophisticated looking, X, photo obviously 10 years old, X, I think that's her dog's photo not hers, X, looks smarter than me, X, etc.

It's depressing, because, as I'm Xing through the list, lonely, lovely women around the state are seeing my photos and thinking: too old, X, ugly dude, X, too educated, X, retired teacher so not rich, X, eats sardines, X, too far away, X, too fat, X, one eye seems to be looking at the other one, X, too hairy, X, etc.

If you send a lady a ☺, then she looks at your photo and description on the site. That's nice. If you don't get a ☺ back, you know she looked you over and said, "Not going to happen, X."

If you text message with someone using the site, the worst thing that happens is ghosting.

You send, "Hi. How are you? I like your picture and that you love hiking and fishing. Would you like to meet sometime for dinner?"

After a week of waiting for a sweet response--*nada*. That's Spanish for "you suck big time, fellow." Then you know you were Xed. It's nothing like the TV X-Games.

The site also allows "blind" dates. The lady's long descriptive attributes are there, but the lady does not include a photo. That earns an **automatic X**. That seems superficial, but isn't appearance our first introduction to the opposite sex? It's why cosmetics, sexy-heeled shoes and beautiful dresses sell so well. Men are supposed to be attracted by looks.

If the texting moves to video-calling, that's fun. Both of the ladies I called on Messenger were pleasant and interesting. And with the camera on the phone or computer they got to show me their houses and pets.

One lady had a two-story home and two cute pups and the other had a four-bedroom, four-bathroom house with pool and two large labs and two cats. I showed each my tiny lanai and my lazy Kitty Blue sleeping on her tower.

DATING DATING

As a new widower, a bachelor again, a single male or whatever you want to call me, I wasn't ready to date for months, but I had been going places with female friends. I called these outings 'no-fault' dates. Hey, I got lonely. Why not just ask a male friend? Well, Sara and I were used to taking a drive around our community in our golf cart each evening, or we'd put the top down on our Miata and drive to the beach to watch the sunset

I just could not hear myself saying:

"Hey, Jake, my man, if there's no football game on, do you want to drive to the beach in my convertible, drink some chardonnay and hold hands while watching the sunset?"

Jake: "Bout time you came out of the closet, Joel!"

Since I haven't dated for 55 years, I'm a little rusty. As a point of clarification, a no-fault date is one where you can go Dutch, not pick your date up at the door, not walk her to the door, and, definitely, not go into her house. Why? Because, for worse or better, depending on the state of your libido, you might wake up the next morning surprised that you're not in bed alone. I've seen a dozen movies where that happened.

Or even, you get up, go to the kitchen to start the coffee and find a woman at the counter smiling and wearing your dress shirt with nothing on underneath. That seems to be an attractive movie scenario too. And the worst, there's a marriage certificate on the bedside table.

So, a no-fault date doesn't involve as much shame or obligation. Being turned down for a no-fault date isn't as bad as being turned down for a date date. Not getting asked out again doesn't produce as much psychological injury for the girl, and, not buying an expensive meal keeps the no-fault date from feeling obligated to give in to a good night kiss or an invitation to come in for a drink.

No fault dates allowed me to break the rule my mother pounded into my teenage stump-like head:

"Joey dear, please don't ever pull up in front of your date's house and honk the horn. It would mortify me if the neighbors heard you do that."

Hey, if a buddy and I go out for lunch, I don't guide him from and to his door with my hand on the middle of his back as if he can't find his own way. I press the horn until he turns down his 70s heavy metal and sticks his head out of the window to curse at me.

These female friends had "guyfriends," as they called them, but two said they were not going to date ever again. At the time, I was trying online dating, which these two roundly 'beat me up' about.

"Just let it happen. You'll meet someone nice in your everyday activities," they advised.

So, I asked:

"Have either of you ever tried dating online?"

Both answered in unison like identical twin sisters:

"Of course!"

The "duh" was unspoken, but the looks I got said it all.

"Oooooookay!" I responded

Ironically, one had told me, when I didn't want to attend one of her friends' gatherings, that:

"Sometimes it's good to get out of your comfort zone."

"Oooooookay!" I responded.

Since I was not ready to switch from no-fault dating to dating dating, yet wanted to have female company, I decide to have "galfriends," the gender equivalent of guyfriends. The term "galfriend" stuck in my throat, though.

"Hey, Jake, my man, I can't take you up on beer-n-bowling tonight because I'm taking a ga ga ga galfriend on a no-fault date to Red Lobster, then Hobby Lobby and Bath and Body Works."

"You drunk, Joel! You're slurring your words. It's pronounced 'girlfriend'. You're going where?"

Time passed and I finally decided to start dating dating. I asked one of my galfriends that I had been having no-fault dates with to go on a date date. She turned me down. I had gotten out of my comfort zone with that request, but the rejection sucked my head back into my shell in an instant like I'd seen hermit crabs do when poked in the eye by a sharp stick wielded by a five-year-old.

When I was a teen calling a girl for a date, my palms would get sweaty, my heart would be a hyper rock star's drums, and my brain worse than compost. The large black, plastic phone receiver would stick to my moist ear and make a sucking sound when I'd pull it loose. I'd lock the door to my dad's den/office so my parents, grandpa and older brothers couldn't hear me. Why lock the door? Even though I'd lower my chin to imitate the bass of a man's voice, occasionally it'd revert to a pre-adolescent soprano for a few syllables. My brothers thought that was hilarious.

If I'd ask my potential date:

"Would you like to go to a movie tonight?"

The fear back then would be to hear the dreaded words:

"I'm sorry, I want to, but I have to wash my hair and put it up for church tomorrow."

Translated, that meant "No, no and NO." What I'd hope for was:

"Yes, Joel, I'd like that."

Second best would be:

"Where are you going?"

That was code for:

"I already told a boy that I had 'to wash my hair,' but If you are going to an out-of-the-way location, I could probably go while avoiding the embarrassing situation of running into the boy I'd rejected earlier."

That would put the ping pong ball back onto my side of the table:

Thinking quickly, I'd say:

"Well, 'The Magnificent Seven' is playing in Kokomo, Noblesville, Elwood and Tipton, so it would be one of those."

"Oh, I want to see that movie, and the Milk Duds at the Kokomo theater are the freshest compared to the other three. I'd love to go."

I would take her to the Kokomo theater and watch whatever was on and eat Jujyfruits. We were both good with that. Hey, she knew the unwritten rules of the game.

Back to "have I had a date date yet?" Nope.

BLOODY NOSE

My nose started bleeding the other day, but not from where you would think. It was up near the bridge. After a couple days of severe pain and daubing with Kleenex, I noticed that a nylon nose pad was missing from my glasses. Aha! The metal nose pad arm was the culprit, attempting to dig a third nostril or burrow a channel for a diamond nose ring I had been lusting over in a jewelry store.

So, I got out my tiny plastic box containing glasses repair items. I knew the screwdriver had both slotted and Philips heads on opposite ends, but, with my glasses off, I couldn't tell which was which until I poked each a couple of times into the soft and tender tissue of my pendulous ear lobe.

In the past when a nose pad fell off, Sara would grab a new one with her delicate, piano-trained fingers, pick up the screw the size of a hair, a red hair I think, and thread it back on by hand, foregoing the use of a screwdriver. She could also thread a needle without spitting on the thread or using one of the tools with a pointed loop of wire that looked like the filament in a lightbulb.

Anyway, I laid out the tools and my glasses and started. My second pair of glasses aren't bifocals, so when I looked at the Lilliputian (the little people in Gulliver's Travels) screw, I saw two of them. I thought back and told myself, "No, you haven't had happy hour yet. It's only 8 am."

It took awhile but I was able to set the screwdriver in the miniature grooves and extract the old screw. I picked a new screw up with my chubby fingers and it disappeared. I couldn't see any of it sticking out anywhere. It was like a bug snuggled in a rug. In fact, when I separated my thumb and forefinger, it was gone. I had done an unintentional magic trick.

I looked on the counter, no! I looked on the floor, no! I didn't see it among the bits of popcorn, potato chips and cookie crumbs beneath the overhang.

Then I looked closely at my thumb. There it was, the clever little rascal, hiding from me under my thumbnail. Aha! I decided I needed Sara's jewelry pliers. I chased the screw around the countertop with the narrow jaws of the little pliers. It reminded me of the time I was trying to retrieve a dropped 20 dollar bill as it leaped and flapped down the sidewalk in a strong breeze. No luck.

Finally, I put a drop of honey on the tips of the pliers. Voilà! That's French for Voilà.

Placing the nylon nose pad on the pad arm, I picked up the screw and searched for the threaded hole. There were two of them, but, since I saw two screws too, my double vision was no problem.

The screw flipped out of my fingers again. I couldn't see it amongst the flotsam and jetsam of my kitchen floor, so I grabbed a painted rooster magnet off the fridge door and ran it across the tile. Nope, nothing on the face of the magnet. I grabbed a flashlight and spent 10 minutes on my hands and knees without success.

I thought I would try the magnet again and, there it was, not on the face but blending in with the feathers on the side of the rooster. As I attempted to pick it up with the honied pliers, it did another flip onto the tile. I was so frustrated I just quit, emptied the dish washer, fried a couple of eggs, put in a load of washing, grumbled a lot and watched a morning news program.

Then I felt something under my heel. I lifted my foot and there was the screw neatly impressed in my flesh alongside a yellow kernel of unpopped popcorn and some beach sand. I then got the screw under control with the pliers, found the hole and screwed it in.

I slathered the entire area with pink nail polish so that the screw wouldn't come out, then, with the assistance of mind-altering polish's acetone swirling in my sinuses, I lay down for a mid-morning nap. I deserved it.

SCROTUM

When our kids were little and we woke up on a leisurely Saturday morning, I'd yell, "Where are my kids?" We could hear Kristin and Mason rustling out of their covers, followed by their bare feet patting the hall floor.

They'd come flying in and bound onto the bed feet first. I taught them quickly the term scrotum, as in "Kids, don't step on daddy's scrotum."

Sara just rolled her eyes, sure that the word would come up in a 4th grade writing assignment, and Child and Family Services would get a call from their teacher.

They knew when my voice went from baritone to a shrill soprano that they had done something that put a damper on my peaceful morning. The sound was attuned to stepping on a pink rubber pig that emits a shrieking whistle from the valve in its belly.

Now, I have a cat, Blue, that likes to walk on my lap while I'm lying reading in bed. Since she has long, sharp claws, I wish she understood the term scrotum

TOOTHPASTE

I hadn't bought toothpaste since Sara passed. I had resorted to simply working through the bathroom drawer that contained a cobblers-dozen of tubes that looked like flattened, upturned elves' shoes.

There were spearmint, peppermint and jalapeno pepper flavors. I may be mistaken about that last one. I googled toothpaste flavors and found this: "The old standbys remain popular, but these days, toothpastes also come in spicy flavors such as fennel or cinnamon-clove, or even in fruit flavors such as apricot or peach."—Oral-B website

Well, the other day I ran out completely. The last tube I finished off by using salad fork tines on the end of the tube and twisting it in a soup spoon, spaghetti-eating style. It was white, peppermint flavored with sand in it.

I hadn't brushed my teeth at the beach lately, so I assumed the sand was meant to be there or was some other abrasive—maybe Comet Cleanser. It reminded me of my childhood with five males and one female using the same bathroom and the same toothpaste.

If no one told the head chandler, Mom, that we were out, we brushed our teeth with baking soda and salt. I liked it and it felt just like the gritty material in my last tube of toothpaste.

I scanned Publix's toothpaste display and was stunned. There were 40 or so different types, some from the same maker. All promised extra white teeth with no gingivitis, plaque, stains, cavities, rotten teeth, bad breath, or mold on your week-old bread.

They came in colors too. One was red and white striped, one blue and white and one came out looking like the American flag. I was trying to buy the one with grit in it again. I couldn't find it.

I ended up buying Colgate Optic White with Charcoal. Its ingredients listed hydrated silica. In other words, watery (hydra) sand (silica). I knew they were using beach material.

It also contained titanium. That must be good. Cellulose. Isn't that from the thighs of young women? Very good. Sodium Lauryl Sulfate. I know Lauryl, he has a brother named Lauryl. Xanax, for panic attacks when you're trying to choose toothpaste. No, wait, it's

Xanthan, not Xanax. Other chemicals I don't want to take time to spell, and blue dye 25 and red dye 781.

Despite the color of those dyes, the paste comes out with black and white stripes. It feels like you have a mouth full of Gold Bond powder but when you spit it's not gold, but dark gray. Luckily, the taste is "cool mint" the package states.

The paste serves double duty. When I have a bonfire in the back yard, I use the charcoal paste as a fire starter.

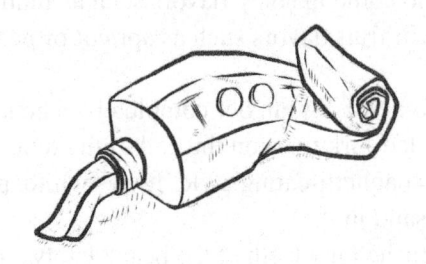

FOR THE LOVE OF CARS!

I once passed a couple picnicking and relaxing in a city park with the gorgeous girl in short shorts and a drop-neck top lying seductively on a blanket. The young man was ten feet away singing country love songs to his Ford Thunderbird. He was also caressing it tenderly with an oversized, sensual cashmere wool mitten. The American Male!

I've known men who've gotten married, had kids, bought a used house trailer for their wife and kids, then built a huge, brand new pole barn for their vehicles.

There was a man who worked in a clothing retail store who complained that he was not making enough money to pay his gas and electric bills. He was driving a truck that had astronomical monthly payments, got 8 miles to a gallon and had giant tires that cost $1,000 apiece. You'd have to have a Tarzan vine or a step ladder for the wife to swing into or climb up to the cab. Let's think, pay for utilities or the truck, utilities or truck, truck or necessities? Truck!

Sam--Hey, Jack. Where should I buy my life insurance? I want to protect my wife and kids if something happens to me?

Jack--I'm not sure, but I think where I get my car insurance they sell house and life insurance.

Sam--Your house isn't insured!

A guy I know had a beautiful crew-cab truck with a plastic bedliner and fiberglass cap the same Sparkle Red as the truck. Once setting up a church yard sale, I suggested we use his truck to pick up some donated items from one of the congregation members' houses. He said, "Oh, I never haul anything in the bed of my truck." I looked over and saw his wife lugging a microwave from the church to a table in the parking lot. I thought, "It's a TRUCK, not a Rolls Royce. Go help your wife, then go trade the truck for a sedan."

I remember trucks that didn't have chrome or anything automatic. They barely had springs. There wasn't even synchromesh for shifting. But there was a key, and you had to put one foot on the brake, a second foot on the clutch, a third foot on the accelerator and a fourth foot to push the springy metal starter button on the floor.

You did this while releasing the hand brake, pulling out the choke knob, steadying the steering wheel and keeping one hand on the three-speed-on-the-floor shifter. If you didn't, shift lever would sometimes snap back and forth then jump out of gear when the engine turned over the first time. So, all you needed were four feet and four hands to start the car.

Now a rough and rugged truck has power windows, power locks, automatic windshield wipers, automatic transmission, shock absorbers, seat belts, AC, heated seats, automatic lumbar adjustment, GPS, motorized mirror adjustment, windshield washers and airbags. If I had a truck, the main feature wouldn't be an airbag, just one windbag.

A commercial plumber friend of mine was giving me a tour of his brand-new truck's features: "Just push this button next to the steering wheel and the car starts. It's like the button on top of our high-end toilets. No car door handle, no toilet handle." For some reason he smiled.

"There are two reservoirs, one for the back window washer and one for the windshield washer. It's like our new Weegood double tank commodes. The water is blue too." He grinned, and I gave him the one-eyebrow-up stare.

"The windshield washer has more pressure than the spritzers on the bidets we put in executives' office suites. Both the driver's and passenger's seats are heated, just like our toilet seats in those suites." I grimaced. When I sit on a toilet seat and it's warm, I check to see if it is also wet. I do the same with taxi and bus seats.

He had a seven-inch plastic button attached in front of one of the A/C-Heater blower vents. I figured it was another expensive gadget.

"What's that?"

"That's the same kind of air freshener we install in gourmet restaurant restrooms." It had the same sticky sweet smell of oily antifreeze that makes your $25 T-bone steak taste like a toilet bowl tablet.

As he was finishing, I fully expected for him to push another button in the back seat, the armrest/cup holder to rise and a two-holer to appear with a roll of Charmin and a Readers' Digest dangling nearby. Or, basically, a Port-a-Potty with an engine and wheels.

Modern American's are truly weird people when it come to their vehicles. They equip their cars with power everything. You can start your car at the touch of a button. You don't even have to wear yourself out taking a heavy key out of your pocket or purse and twisting it in the ignition.

I also watched a friend open the tailgate of her minivan with just a lift of her foot. At first I thought she kicked the bumper to make the hatch open, the way Fonzie would smack the Coke machine to make a free pop clank down the chute. That would have been cool.

With all the energy Sara and I saved over the years by not walking around the car locking with a key, reaching down to unlatch the back hatch, cranking up and down windows, washing our windshield by hand or shifting gears, we ended up joining a the Fitness Center to push another button and pay to run in-place.

From left to right: clutch pedal, dimmer button (above), brake pedal, accelerator pedal, starter button and three-foot gear shift lever.

THESE EASE EAT

If you've traveled south of the border, you probably know that "These ease eat" means "This is it." The problem is *these, ease* and *eat* are English words that don't mean *this, is* or *it*.

Spanish and many other languages are phonetic, and in Spanish "i" is pronounced ee.

On the other hand, we use English, a confusing mishmash of languages so that *fish* can be spelled using the made-up word "ghoti." That's right:

- gh as the f sound in rouGH

- o as the i sound in wOmen

- ti as the sh sound in naTIon

Just think how hard it is to learn English when we have exceptions to every rule.

Many years ago, Sandy McIntyre of KGC was active in the Sarasota County Literacy Council and talked me into becoming a tutor for immigrants.

She knew that I had taught English in high school and also was a TEFL (Teaching English as a Foreign Language) volunteer in the Peace Corps after I retired. So, becoming an ESL (English as a Second Language) tutor would be as easy as spilling my notes off a lectern.

Teaching foreigners for years introduced me to residents of Azerbaijan and immigrants from Russia, Ukraine, Haiti, Colombia, Mexico and Puerto Rico. Plus, Sara and I encountered lots of confusing foreign terms in our many international travels.

While teaching at Khazar University, Azerbaijan, I asked one of my students what his name meant. He said, "Eunuch." Nah! No parent would name their son for a castrated male.

I had to have heard wrong, so I shook my head to loosen any earwax, turned my good ear to him and asked him to repeat the synonym for his name. "Eunuch." I had heard him correctly.

I prodded further. When he tried to give me other synonyms, such as, *one, sole* or *lone*, it took me a while to realize that he was trying to pronounce *unique*.

That's u-NIQUE not EU-nuch. Where you placed the accent was important.

While in Azerbaijan, son Mason and his wife visited me. I lived in the Caucus Mountains, but the international airport was near Baku five hours away through the desert. We splurged on returning to Baku from Shaki by hiring a taxi.

In Azerbaijan, the men believe that a good driver is a fast driver. Our trip included narrow roads, driving through herds of sheep, passing donkey carts, playing chicken with tiny Russian-made Ladas and crossing some dry mountains.

Mason was in the front seat, and the Mercedes was skittering down the road so fast I swear the tires only touched the ground occasionally. Now I knew why the driver had thrown a few coins into a box at a religious shrine beside the road to prepay for driving like the devil.

From the back seat I tried to tell the driver to slow down, so I yelled in Azerbaijani, *"Lavash lavash."* I realized later that I was yelling, "Bread bread." He looked in the back seat and gave me a raised eyebrow and pushed the accelerator clear to the floor. He must have thought I was starving to death. The correct words were *yavash yavash*, slowly slowly.

All speakers in the world take shortcuts with language. In other words, they don't enunciate. I was trying to get my students to speak English rapidly, so I asked them what *daday* meant in English.

Of course, there is no such word. But we often say, "How ya do'n daday."

Try it. Say, "How are you doing today" so that each sound is enunciated clearly, then say it the way you do every day. It's just one of many pronunciations, such as, *gonna, wanna, hava*, that drive foreigners whacky when they try to look them up in their dictionary.

One of my Azeri students kept using *whisit* in her writing and speech. I told her: "There was no such word in English. Is it a new kitchen or cleaning gadget advertised on TV?"

"Whisit! Like, my uncle came to whisit us last night." Then I remembered that many Europeans and Latinos pronounce v differently. When I was in Havana, Cuba, *Havana* was pronounced *Habana*. So *very* may come out *berry*.

Uh, or schwa (ə), is the most used vowel sound in the English language. Sadly, for those speaking other languages, they have not learned the uh sound and have never had to create it. It's like Americans trying to pronounce the German r or trill the Spanish double r.

Many foreign schools teach that *uh* is pronounced with a relaxed jaw, from deep in the throat and is a quiet and simple grunt. Those who mimic English speech say American English sounds like: "Nuh, nuh, NUH, nuh, NUH, nuh, nuh, nuh, NUH, nuh, NUH, nuh ..."

So, *money* can come out *moony* and, since in Spanish (español) *e* proceeds *st* and *sp* in their words, *state* can come out estate, as in Estados Unidos (States United). The confusion comes because, again, *moony* and *estate* are English words.

On a bus trip through England and Ireland, we made a restroom stop and I sat on a stone wall waiting for everyone to come out. When I got off the wall and returned to the bus, Sara was brushing off the seat of my pants.

"What are you doing?" I asked.

"Honey, you have dust on your fanny."

An Australian lady on the bus looked shocked and discretely shushed her. I guess in colloquial language "down under," Sara had proclaimed, "Joel, you have dust on your female genitals." Surprised me on several levels!

I WAS SHOT IN THE MALL

I guess that's better than being shot in the rump. Anyway, I was shot twice in the arm at Sarasota Square Mall all in one month. Of course, I can't blame the officials because I was wearing a mask. In fact, when I enter a bank, it seems the teller are giving all of us in masks a second look.

Like most, I'm still struggling with the mask protocol. I don't know how many times I have left my car, walked toward a store and turned around after seeing someone enter with a mask. Slumping back to the car I go. I usually have a fresh one in the glove compartment and a gently used one hanging from the heater knob.

Once I was shopping in Publix and finished except for getting my prescriptions. I was conversing with the pharmacist when I realized that my mask was on wrong. The young lady probably wondered why my beard was so precious that it was the only part of my face the mask protected.

I'm not alone with that, because I've seen people only cover their lips, leaving their nose and nostrils uncovered. The other day at euchre, Judi Doucette had her mask attached to her elbow. She claims masks work, since her elbow has not come down with a case of Covid-19 yet.

Those who are fashion conscious but also following CDC recommendations often swagger toward a store with their mask at the ready, either dangling nonchalantly from one ear, tucked into their shirt like a priest's collar or neatly folded worn around their neck like a bow tie. Of course, then there are the teens that duck in their heads and pull their T-shirt over their nose and breathe through a print of Ice Cube.

At least the CDC now tells us that if we've had both shots we can dine outside maskless with friends. I went out for fish and chips with David Westbrook at Dockside Waterfront Grill the other day. I only wore my mask while walking through the restaurant onto a patio and back out to the car. Everyone there seemed fine with that.

There are several problems with how masks function. When I'm conducting presentations at Oscar Scherer State Park, I will give masks to visitors who forgot theirs. I notice people wearing the blue side in, snapping one of the rubber bands, holding the broken band up to one ear, or sporting their mask upside down with the adjustable nose clip giving them a pointy chin.

I had to visit my doctor the other day, so I put on my mask, saw the doctor and took the mask off on the way out. I had been warned that the mask elastic often tangles with the nylon tubes on a hearing aid. When I reached the car and stored my mask, I realize both hearing aids had been flipped off. I conducted a forensic investigation of the inside and outside of the car with no luck.

Finally, I walked back into the office and found one right at the door, but the other one was still missing. I told the receptionist my dilemma and asked if anyone had found one.

"No, where did you lose it."

"I don't know. That's why I'm asking you."

"Did you hear it hit the floor?"

"No, because I didn't have my hearing aids on."

Though I couldn't hear clearly as I walked away, she said something else non-nonsensical that sounded like, "Oel smar tass." Ha, those aren't even real words.

I went back across the driveway to the parking spots, sure that the little rascal was on the pavement. Just then a UPS truck comes rumbling along to make a delivery. I waved for him to stop—I didn't want to see half of my $5,000 auditory investment turn in to flesh-colored powder under the truck wheels.

He stopped, got out and we walked bent over for 10 minutes scanning every imbedded seashell, smashed cigarette filter, smudge of Juicy Fruit chewing gum, shiny pop tab and a variety of small stones.

We gave up and I got back into my car. I put on my seat belt and felt a dull pain right over my heart. What next! A heart attack? I grabbed my chest. There in my left pocket was the hearing aid. It had flipped off my ear, probably done a couple of somersaults in the air and landed in my shirt pocket.

On the way home I stopped at Arby's for a sandwich. When I walked in with my mask on, the place stank to high heavens. I walked up to the counter and could hardly get my breath.

I wondered, "What is that dead fish smell?" Then I remembered I had reused the mask I wore after eating fish and chips several days early. I guess I wasn't eating fresh.

A POKER LESSON

In 1968 BC (before children) Sara and I used to get together with another couple and a friend to play poker. It was dealer's choice, so the beers we were drinking made the evening way more confusing than a night of Sprite and euchre.

Years passed and I ran into a Texas hold'em tournament on TV, and it looked like fun. But I never played even though my 55+ community has several poker nights. After 9 years, I finally sat down with six other people for a Friday night game.

I'd only played poker at a kitchen table, so a real poker table was a surprise. There were built-in chip trays and stainless-steel cups for poker chips, drinks, or a second deck of cards. Jeannine had her keys in hers. I was hoping we weren't playing for golf carts. Since there were no drinks at the table, I poured my bag of Peanut M&Ms in mine. The metallic clatter made everyone jerk and look up.

"Oops. Sorry!"

I knew people at poker tables spoke a foreign language. I just didn't know how foreign. I had heard a little bit of it when watching TV poker, but that didn't mean I understood. My opponents were patient with me, though.

Lorie dealt the cards and Bob said, "Joel, you're on the button."

"Oops, sorry." So, I stood up and looked for it on my chair.

"No, it means you're the dealer," explained Jean. I just stared at her with my eyebrows raised, because I had just seen Lorie deal and no button was in sight. She pointed to a red Tiddlywink on the table in front of me. That didn't help, but they went on anyway, several talking at the same time.

"Ilene is the small blind and Tim is the big blind," I picked out from Bob's voice among the noise of others trying to clarify.

I didn't think it was nice to call people names, but Tim and Ilene each had a Tiddlywink of their own, and for some reason, they took the insult without rancor. Bob explained that the biggest blind had to bet blindly.

What! Why were we punishing Tim? His Tiddlywink had Big Blind written on it too—labeled like the letter A on Hester's dress in the novel Scarlet Letter.

Tim tossed two white chips onto the table.

"What's the smaller blind Tiddlywink mean?" I asked, wondering what Ilene's punishment was.

"It means that I have to bet blindly too, but, if I throw my hand into the muck, I only have to put in one chip," explained Ilene. "Otherwise, I put in two."

When I was a kid on the farm, I'd put on my mucking boots, and scoop manure out of the barn. I didn't see where the muck was, but maybe it was in the restroom.

I looked down and exclaimed, "I only have two cards."

"I know," said Lorie. "You can use the five cards face down on the table to make a hand."

Great! I scooped all of them up, and, sure enough, I had a really good hand. Everyone at the table was wide-eyed.

"No, no, no!" came from all corners. "We'll show you," offered Karin as she nodded to Lorie, who was holding a fresh deck of cards.

Lorie dealt again, but I still only received two cards. Karin firmly put her hand over the five cards in the middle of the table and gave me the "teacher" eye, meaning, *don't you even think about it, buddy*.

That's when the rules and language became even more complicated.

TO BE CONTINUED

A POKER LESSON continued

"What are the chips worth?" I asked

"The white ones are 1; the red, 2; the blue, 5; the green, 20; and the black, 50," explained Lorie.

"Okay, so let me get this straight. The ones that have nothing printed on them are 1, the ones that read 5 are 2, 10s are 5, 25s are 10, and 100s are 50?" I repeated to make sure I had heard correctly.

"You'll catch on," encouraged Bob.

"Good, but I have one more question. One, two, five what? Dollars, pennies, what?"

"Just one, two, etc."

Everyone looked at the two cards in their hand.

Lorie said, "Karin, you're under the gun." I thought of the Old West. Isn't this a friendly game? Is someone pointing a gun at her under the table. I finally guessed that meant she would bet first.

"Check," says Karin.

So, I checked everyone out and noticed nothing weird. Jean checked, Lorie checked, Bob checked and I bet the maxim, two something-or-others. Ilene threw in, Tim, Karin, Jean, Lorie and B0b did too.

"No one staying with him?" asked Bob. "I guess you win, Joel."

Wow! That was easy. I didn't understand "staying with him," though, maybe he knew my daughter and son-in-law had been at my house the day before. Kind of a non sequitur, I thought.

The next four hands were similar, except different people had the Tiddlywinks in front of them. All I had to do was look at my cards, throw some chips on the table, they threw their chips out with mine and I scooped them up and sorted them into my chip tray. Then I would eat a couple of Peanut M&Ms.

"You must be getting good 'hole cards'," said Tim. Is he saying I have cards in a hole in the chair or the table? Does that mean he thinks I'm cheating? I gave him the questioning eye.

"That's the two cards you don't show. Also, called the pocket cards," Tim explained. Did people put a card in the hole in their pocket?

I won the next hand and Ilene said, "Bluff." Did poker players just yell out random words after a win like "hurrah," "bravo" or "olé"? I decided that after winning a hand I would follow the "bluff" term trend and call out, "cliff," "overhang," "crag," "ridge," or "escarpment."

Karin said with a grin, "Are you bluffing?" I raised my eyebrows, and she went on. "Betting big with a poor hand to make us drop out."

I had not been bluffing, since my hands were something like this: Ace, nine; king, queen; 7 and 8 of hearts; 10, queen; and so forth. Even when I had a weak 7, 8 suited hand, the first cards turned face up would include an 8 or 7, giving me a pair. It was crazy luck that confused my opponents.

Finally, I lost a hand with two queens.

Tim laid down twos and said, "Ducks."

Bob said, "Cowboys," and flipped over kings.

Ducks and cowboys? What's next, giraffes and policemen?

As Lorie dealt, she talked. When she put down three cards in the middle of the table she said, "Here's the flop," then after we bet, one more card, "the turn," more betting, then the last card of the five, "the river." I knew some Spanish and Turkish, but now I was learning the language of Texas.

I also noticed that Lorie was doing an underhanded deal. She'd put down a couple of cards, then slip two on the bottom of the deck, then another card and two more on the bottom of the deck.

I didn't like that, so I called her out on it: "You're dealing from the bottom of the deck or something," and everyone looked up from their hand.

"She is burning those cards," explained Bob. I didn't understand, maybe she saw some chocolate smudges from the M&Ms I kept eating and was going to burn the cards with the trash. Anyway, everyone seemed to think burning cards was normal.

We played, and I received a refresher on what would win besides three of a kind, two pair or ace high. I finally asked, "Remind me of what's above four aces and straights."

"Royal flush," offered Jean. The only image I could come up with was Queen Elizabeth, while sitting stiffly on the "throne" in deep concentration, with a handmaiden waiting patiently to pull the golden royal chain of the commode. A Royal Flush.

My luck held out for the rest of the evening, and I won big. I had to thank them for being helpful with a rookie. Plus, after two hours, I was throwing around such terms as "bullets," "gut shot," "kicker," "limp in," "nuts," "inside straight," "tank" and "tilt" with the rest of them.

FINALLY DATING

I'm finally dating. Sara and I talked a lot about what we should do if one of us passed, and we both said that the other should live again, love again, and have adventures again. Of course, there will never be anyone in my life like Sara, but I'm dating Nancy Brown from my community. She's one of a kind too, not a replacement, but her lovely self.

I chuckle at the name Nancy Brown, because it's hard to introduce her. Here are some of the interactions:

Me: "Bill, I'd like you to meet Nancy Brown."

Bill: "Ha ha, you kidder. I suppose you're calling yourself Joe Smith or John Jones, now. Come on. What's her real name? You can't keep her identity a secret from me, you rascal."

Me: "Linda, this is Nancy Brown."

Linda: "I had a roommate in college named Nancy Brown. Alpha Sigma Delta Lambda Tau Epsilon. Short round girl, with freckles and a brain like a clutch purse. Aced every history test. And when………"

Me: "I want you to meet my friend Nancy Brown, Ailene."

Ailene: "I loved my Aunt Nancy Brown. When she was younger, she looked just like you."

Me: "Sam, have you met Nancy Brown."

Sam: "Hey, I used to date you in high school. Remember? About 50 years ago. Back at Roosevelt High in Peoria, Illinois."

Nancy: "No, I lived in Connecticut. I've never been to Illinois."

Sam: "Oh, must be another Nancy Brown."

The name Nancy is ranked 11th in popularity right now, while Joel doesn't even make the top 100 EVER. *Nancy* is graced with two resonant nasal consonants, while I've had *Joel* spelled *Jowl* because W is one key left of E on computers and fat fingers stray.

Nancy means "gracious." Joel, on the other hand, means "Jehovah is Lord." Take that, Nancy Brown!

There are about 1,000,000 Nancys in America. Joel doesn't even rank in the top 200. Brown ranks 4th even on a rainy hump day at work in a cubicle, while Robbins ranks 366th only if it's a sunny day at the beach in summer.

Oh, well!

TEA TREE

Well, the other day I was looking through Sara's bathroom cabinet and remembered that I had filled a red plastic crate with her melon-cucumber body sprays, balsam splashes, tea tree oil, apple blossom shower gels, aloe vera mint lotions, vanilla sugar and other powders and liquids. I pulled out the four that were on top. They were labeled B & B warm melon-cucumber silky smooth toiletries. Well, I was NOT going to go around smelling like a cucumber or its cousin, the zucchini, anytime soon. So, what should I do?

The tea tree oil went into my basket of Tetley orange pekoe, Tazo mint and Lipton green tea. I figured it would add a unique flavor to my morning hot drinks. I set the four melon-cucumber bottles on my kitchen counter. The vanilla sugar I put with my brown sugar, powdered sugar, raw granulated sugar and baking flour.

When girlfriend Nancy Brown came over to go kayaking, I gave her the four melon-cucumber bottles, and she started giggling.

She exclaimed, "Here you gave me this beautiful, expensive set of fragrances, and I brought you a can of Anti-Monkey Butt powder. It's because you had been complaining about underarm and thigh chafing due to wet swimming suits and working in the yard wearing sweaty clothes."

Everyone has a chafing dish. Well, remember that underarm chafing is a completely different animal.

Chuckling, I told her: "Why couldn't you just have brought me some Gold Bond or talcum powder!"

I went to my medicine cabinet to store--read that hide--the Anti-Monkey Butt powder in case a guest used my bathroom. The cabinet was where I stored the unused items given to me in my Peace Corps volunteer emergency medical kit. It was set up to provide for physical problems while I served in the jungles of Liberia. I placed the Anti-Monkey Butt Powder container behind an unopened box of Preparation H suppositories. Wait, that wasn't any better. So, I shuffled through the jungle supplies and found athlete's foot and toenail fungus ointments. Nope! Finally, I hid it behind a large box of rehydration powder. That was tame enough.

Often weird things happen when I'm with Nancy. When her daughter Katherine was visiting recently, we went out to eat at Thai Bistro, drank plum wine and ate Asian food before going to Venice Beach to watch the sunset. There they sipped a little more wine, but I didn't because I was driving, and driving Nancy's Toyota RAV 4 to boot. It is much different from my little Miata convertible. We were driving home down Venice Avenue and, when I turned onto Pinebrook, the streetlights were fewer. Seeing the road was difficult, and I wondered if I had mistakenly missed turning on the headlights.

I fiddled around with the switches and turned off all the exterior lights. The road went cat black, and I heard Nancy and Katherine gasp. I quickly rotated the knob to what appeared to be parking lights, switched to what I hoped were the regular lights, then flipped on the high beams. An oncoming car menacingly blinked its high beams back several times.

I twisted the knob quite a few times before I was sure which setting was right. As I was driving and cycling from no lights through different levels, my speed reached 43 in the 30-mph zone. Nancy reminded me that the police gave lots of tickets between Venice Avenue and Edmundson Road. "You don't want to get pulled over, Joel."

I noticed a car tailgating us, but I slowed down anyway, hoping it wouldn't rear-end us. Just then I was blinded by lights.

We were lit up with a spotlight and flashing blue and red lights on a Venice police cruiser. When the policeman approached the car cautiously—hand on gun--to see what swerving, light blinking, speeding, possibly drunk, feasibly gun toting and maybe dangerous maniac was behind the wheel of the SUV, we all broke out laughing.

He probably wondered if we were all inebriated, because I had been randomly turning on and off my lights. But he heard my excuses that it wasn't my car, and I had been trying to find the headlights while attempting to slow to the speed limit. Evidently, he smelled nothing on my breath more potent than spicy Thai chicken curry, took my license and Nancy's registration, said the speed limit was actually a little low on that street, and sent us on our way.

We all three looked into the rearview mirrors and watched the policeman walk back to his car shaking his head vigorously. That made us rock in our seats and cover our mouths with our hands. We had to hurry home because we were each afraid we would not reach the safety of a bathroom quickly enough.

ALL OF A SUDDEN

Let's say at one time, Sara had been washing clothes and came up from the basement and told me the dryer wasn't working. I could get up at 7:30 the next day, ride my bike four miles to school, teach till noon, ride my Schwinn to Ace to pick up a dryer belt while eating a sack lunch, be back in the classroom at 12:30, teach till 3, supervise the stage set crew preparing for the senior play until 5:30, ride home, shoot baskets in the driveway with the kids, talk school when Sara got home from teaching, put the kids to bed and then go to the basement and tear the dryer apart and replace the belt. Then I could go over my next day's class preparations and drop into bed at 12.

Now that I'm retired and have 24 hours of unscheduled time, it takes me 3 or 4 days to trim the bushes in front of the house, a 45-minute job. What's my "really busy" retiree's day like? I wake up at 7 am, decide that I will do the trimming early before it gets too hot and humid.

When my snooze control goes off the third time, I get up at 7:40, feed Kitty Blue, dip chunks out of her litter box, put seven dollars' worth of seed in the bird feeder, fix a cup of coffee and drink it on the lanai while watching Cherie, Jan, Don, Tony, Rich, Lisa and others walk dogs, ride bikes or stroll by.

All of a sudden it's 9. Then girlfriend Nancy calls and asks if I've had breakfast. No? Come on over. I drink another cup of coffee on her lanai, we point out the joints all over our bodies that ache, chat about the drama of our neighbors, kids and grandkids, and fix and eat breakfast. All of a sudden it's 11 am. Oops!

I speed home in my golf car and call the students I tutor online using Facebook's video chat app Messenger. They're in Baku, Azerbaijan, where it's 7 pm.

I say, "Good morning, Inji and Khalil," and they respond, "Good evening, Mr. Joel."

Lessons end at 12 noon, I pay bills, check my email, unload the dishwasher, and load the clothes washer.

All of a sudden it's 1 pm and nap time. I stretch out on my bed, play a computer word game, lose one hand of digital solitaire, and slog through online euchre with people from Michigan and Australia, then read a few chapters of a Hemingway novel before dozing off.

Bam! All of a sudden, it's 2:30. It's too hot to trim the bushes, so I go to the pool and gossip with Rod, John, Nancy, Tony, Val and others. All of a sudden it's 4:30, and we've been talking about Captain Eddie's fried oysters, Publix's sushi, Bogey's supreme pizza, Mad Moe's juicy hamburgers, Dairy Queen's onion rings, Thai Bistro's curry and Dockside Grill's shrimp cocktail. I'm hungry.

I tell Nancy to come over for happy hour. We open a bottle of wine, snack on crackers and cheese, and all of a sudden it's 6. We order a pizza to be delivered. Nancy reminds me that I have to logon to Whatsapp to video tutor Victoria, who's originally from Mexico, at 8.

At 9:10 pm we start a movie and, Kitty Blue, the traitor, crawls onto Nancy's lap. We watch with at least one eye still open--most of the time--while Blue sleeps purring.

All of a sudden it's 11:30, and Nancy shakes me awake, pops out of a La-Z-Boy, and tells me she is departing for home.

Unbelievably, all of a sudden, the day's gone. Before I go to sleep, I decide that tomorrow morning I will trim the bushes before it gets too hot and humid.

MY OLYMPICS

The Olympic games are dominating my thoughts and time right now. Sara loved to watch Synchronized Swimming, where teams of women lift only their delicate feet out of the water, point them skyward and wiggle their toes. Now I tend to watch only those events that are violent and include a chance of blood.

Don't you love viewing pole vaulting, waiting for the pole to snap and the athlete to twist out of danger. Or, anticipate a competitor in the hammer throw letting loose too soon and tossing it into the scrambling crowd. I wonder what they pay the judges who stand down field while the javelin contestants throw spears at them. Not enough, I bet.

I'm amazed at the skill displayed by all the athletes, and I'm also jealous.

Could there be a sport, out of the many new ones, that I could participate in? I beat out 40+ competitors in my retirement community to win the club shuffleboard championship one year. I saw synchronized diving and thought, how about synchronized shuffleboard. Nope, not on the list.

Last night I saw a list of Tokyo Olympic finals that would be shown on NBC later. One coming up was air rifles and pistols. I searched in my closet for my Daisy Red Ryder lever action BB gun and practiced shooting Campbell soup cans at the club's five acres. That prepared me for watching.

Well, the air guns they were shooting looked like slim-line Dyson vacuum sweepers. They were shooting 10 meters, while my BBs would begin a drooping trajectory at about 10 feet.

Skeet shooting would be more interesting if instead of clay pigeons they used the live blackbirds that leave white droppings on my Miata. Plus, if the birds flew toward the spectator stands, shots in that direction would give the audience some practice in "duck and run."

I saw Street Skateboarding made it into the Olympics this year. So, I watched about a half hour and decided it was improperly named. It should be called Street Tumbling, Taking Dumb Chances,

Intentional Neutering, trying to earn a Darwin Award, or Training for EMTs.

Hey, I've shot arrows, so maybe I could compete in archery. I still have a bow. It's one-piece fiberglass. Then I looked at the Olympic ones. They looked like my neighbor's pole-mounted weather station. There were gadgets sticking out all over. They even had sights.

All the swimming events made me envious. I have trouble walking up the steps out of the pool without falling back in, let alone trying a hundred-meter medley.

Instead of the event taekwondo, how about tie-my-shoe competitions. Bending over is painful. I have to use a three-foot shoehorn even for my flip flops.

One event that was to be shown was the Men's Individual Epee. Now there's one I wanted to see! I've heard of email, ecommerce, e-banking and e-books. When I tuned in, I was disappointed to find out the event was fencing. Swords! Well, my farm boy buddies and I participated in the youthful sport of e-peeing that involved fencing too. Electric fencing.

We challenged each other to see how long we could stand there without screaming. The answer: Not long.

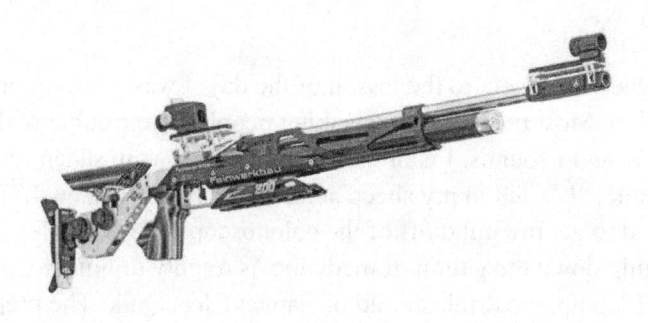

V AND B SOUNDS

I help a young lady from Mexico improve her English, and I had to explain to her that we would need to skip a lesson because I had a medical procedure that would interfere with our video tutoring time slot. Basically, after I drank the Clenpiq colonoscopy medicine at 7 pm, I would be indisposed for our 8 pm appointment.

She seemed concerned and asked, "What wrong?"
My mind searched through my understanding and vocabulary for appropriate words.

"I'm having a colonoscopy done."

"What that?"

"In Spanish, it's *colonoscopia*."

"Que? What?"

I was thinking that I could say, "It's where a doctor sedates you and sticks a camera and flashlight up…" But that was too implausible and gross sounding.

"Es la forma en que examinan su colon en busca de problemas con el uso de instrumentos. It's how they examine your colon for problems using instruments."

"Ay ay ay!"

"I know!"

I changed the subject to the lesson of the day. I was working on pronunciation. Most non-English speaking people have trouble with the uh, V, W and I sounds. I is often pronounced ee, as in sheep for ship. Example, "I sailed in my sheep across the English Channel."

I wanted to get my mind off of the colonoscopy prep, which after you gulp down the gallon of medicine, is mighty draining. Instead of Clenqip, the drink should be named CleanQuik. The prep makes you sprint to the bathroom.

So, I read a sentence and had my student mimic my pronunciation.

Me: "This is a very large bowl of soup. Please repeat."
Student: "These ease a bwary large bowel of soup."

"Well, It's not <u>ease</u>, it's <u>is</u>. It's not <u>bwary</u>, it's <u>very</u>. And, it's not <u>bowel</u>, it's definitely <u>bowl</u>. Bowel in Spanish means *intestino*.

We don't want to say we're giving someone a large intestine of soup."

She laughed.

Nooo! My mind was back on my colonoscopy.

So, I switched to another lesson, an easy way to know how to pronounce words ending in a silent E.

I told her: "<u>Bit</u> when a silent E is added becomes <u>bite</u>, <u>not</u> becomes <u>note</u>, <u>tub</u> becomes <u>tube</u>, and <u>can</u> becomes <u>cane</u>. With the silent E added, the pronunciation is the same as the vowel's names, A E I O U. We call that a long vowel sound."

"I no understand."

"If an E is added to the word <u>bar</u>, the A sound is long. <u>Bare</u>. Understand?"

"So a E make bowel long, just like name, A E I O U. Right?"

Nooo! We were again back on colons, intestines and "long" bowels.

"You're right, but, again, it's not <u>bowel</u>, it is <u>vowel</u>!"

Since I could not seem to change the subject, I gave up and cut the lesson short as soon as I could.

ALARMED

Because of a pending colonoscopy, I had been up most of the night the other day with a gallon jug of a diarrhea cocktail in one hand and my other hand clutching the grab bar next to the toilet seat I was firmly attached to.

Anyway, I slept in the day after the colonoscopy, getting up at 9 am, eating breakfast and sitting on the lanai leisurely drinking a cup of coffee. Then the phone rang.

It was my girlfriend Nancy. We exchanged pleasantries, but I could tell something was amiss.

"Ok. What's wrong?"

"Well, all the neighbors on my street are outside checking their car alarms, looking at their neighbors' cars, and walking around their houses in a state of confusion."

"Aaaand?"

I love Nancy, but she seldom answers a question immediately. It's like tweezing a splinter out of your finger. You have to keep digging.

"There's an incessant beep-beep coming from under my living room."

"Aaaand?"

"I have a sump pump under my house with an alarm that goes off if it fails. It's beeping."

"Aaaand?"

"I don't know how to stop it, but it's upsetting everyone. With the constant beep-beep beep-beep, I'm annoying my neighbors, and it's annoying me."

"Aaaaand?

"What should I do?"

"There you go! I knew you could do it."

"There's some water coming out of the outside pipe, but it's usually more. Maybe the pipe's clogged."

By then the caffeine in my mug had pushed the last remnants of the previous day's anesthesia from my brain.

"Give me a minute and I'll come over. Do you have a snake?"

"You know I don't have a snake. I don't like snakes. I called the office to tell them it wasn't a Medalert beeper or my car alarm, so not to be alarmed."

"Good idea. I don't have a snake either. I'm on my way."

"Good to know. Thanks."

When I arrived with a spool of wire and some electrician's pliers, I noticed Gigi at the end of the street excitedly pushing buttons on her key fob, which was aimed at her car like a loaded Glock.

Nancy came out and I bent a hook on the end of the wire and snaked it up the five feet to the elbow where the outlet pipe ran under the house. No debris came out. So, I took the garden hose and tried to flush material out of the pipe. Nothing.

"There's a button on the alarm that disarms it. It's way under the house."

"Aaaand?"

"Someone has to crawl under there and push the button."

"I've got two metal knees. So, I'm begging off."

"I'll go," she said as she went into the house.

My esteem for Nancy rose several notches but was she serious? There are creepy crawly roaches, amphibians and spiders in most crawlspace swamps. Then she came out of the house a couple minutes later in full-length jeans and a long-sleeved T-shirt.

I removed one wire-covered decorative cement block, which was the access point to the crawl space and in she went. I watched as the multicolored soles of her Nike's disappeared into the dark abyss. After a few minutes of huffing and puffing, she yelled.

"I pushed the button."
"Ok. The beeping has stopped."
"The float is stuck up."
"Jiggle it."
"Ok. It came down."

She wiggled out and I replaced the concrete block. She had muddy elbows, knees, forehead, tummy and tip of nose. We were basking in mission accomplished.

Then she asked, "Should I have turned the alarm back on?"

As I stood there clean as a licked spoon, I was afraid to respond to her question. Nancy's not the only one who sometimes doesn't answer immediately.

CHRISTMAS DANCING: Salsa, Rumba, Cha-cha, Merengue, Samba, Bossa Nova & Tango

My son knew that fiancée Nancy and I were going to dances. I had written about trying to learn the Cupid Shuffle, jitterbug, box step and Electric Slide. But I didn't expect to receive a dance-oriented Christmas present from my son's family.

The box was nicely wrapped, so Ernante had probably tied the bows and not Mason. Mason's behind me and says Forest wrapped it. Where was Remy? The square container was about five inches tall when unwrapped and labeled Rumba, so I was excited. A new dance for us.

I, especially, needed practice, because I had pretty well bruised all of Nancy's toes, and, unless she bought steel-toed work boots to dance in, she would soon be a cripple.

What was in the box? I figured it would be a large plastic sheet, kind of like Twister's pad, rows of red, blue, yellow, and green circles. Instead of plate-sized circles, though, I thought it would feature shoeprint patterns for foot placement and arrows for directions.

The box was too big for that, so I was hoping it also had an inflatable buxom blonde, with elastic bands on her feet that would fit over my shoes. Then anyone peeking into my windows at night would be impressed with how suave I was.

To my surprise, the box contained a heavy disk. It had a button on top that I pushed.

It said: "I Robot."

I responded: "I Joel."

Before I could react, away it went. Little antennas were flicking out, I assumed, to sense for delicate digits sticking out of open-toed ladies' dancing shoes.

In a flash, I caught up with it and jumped on top to see how this rumba robot would take me through the motions of the famous South American dance. No luck. It squatted and stopped.

Just then Mason walked in and asked: "What the heck are you doing?"

"Learning the rumba. What did you expect?"

"The rumba! You're crushing it. And, it's not rumba, it's Roomba."

"That's what I said, "Rumba."

"Get off!"

He explained that it was a vacuum sweeper and that my La-Z-Boy would no longer have to have popcorn kernels and peanut hulls scattered around it like New Year's confetti when company came.

He reset the vacuum and set it in motion. It found one of the cat's ping pong balls and batted it back and forth with Kitty Blue for a few seconds until Blue made a GOOOAALLL between two chair legs. Then it went around picking up cat hair, sock lint, cracker crumbs, hairballs, orange Cheeto powder and other flotsam and jetsam.

> No new dance step for me, but I have a cool Roomba bumping and grinding around the house.

Behind Bars

Well, I made an appointment at Publix for 5:50 pm to get my Covid-19 booster shot. Instead of driving, I decided to walk on the multiple-use-path (MUP) along Honoré. I worked up a good sweat getting there ahead of time and was greeted with, "Did you make an appointment?"

"Yes."

"You don't have an appointment in the computer."

"Yes, I do, because I made it Monday for Venezia Plaza Publix."

"It's not in here," she said, looking at the computer. "Do you have the confirmation."

"No, I just printed out the checklist sheet and filled it out so I could be early and ready."

"Sorry."

"Great system you have there! Well, how about a walk-in, then."

"No. The schedule is full. We can book you in an hour."

I started to sweat again as the heat in me was rising.

"Great, I walked over here, so I don't have time to walk home and walk back, so, NO."

"The pharmacist came over, said, "Wait, that man over there was our 6 o'clock and he's here now, can you wait till 6?"

"Yes."

They were very efficient, so I also received my flu shot and headed back home to play euchre at 7 o'clock.

When I reached the gate, again in a sweat, my white pass card wouldn't work. I swiped, banged, tapped and rubbed it all over the sensor without luck. Here I was, it was completely dark, looking like I was homeless, locked out of my own community. That eliminated Plan A.

Plan B: Climb the gate because the wall was too high. Then I looked at the pointy, spear-like ends of each post. Plus, I didn't think my fat, old leg would reach to the top bar anyway.

Plan C: I called Rod, always a friend of the needy and locked out, and asked him to drive over to let me in with the gate code chip on his window.

"Can't. Remember, won't open from the inside because a part's back ordered."

"&%#$, right!"

Before we figured out he could drive down King Arthur, cross the bridge, on out to King's Way to Laurel Road to Honoré to open the gate, Lonney and Della pulled up and the gate opened.

"Thank heavens," I exclaimed.

"Sorry, it's illegal to let you in, you know."

Plan D: I sprinted ahead of their Mini Cooper and through the gate with all three of us laughing all the way.

NOT GLAMPING AT A STATE PARK

I hadn't been camping for 20 years, when Nancy said, "Let's go camping," I remembered how much fun it was 30 years ago. That's pre back surgery and two artificial knees for me and two hip replacements for Nancy. Pre arthritis too.

"Let's do it, but let's make it simple," I huffed. "No U-Hall full of dishes, propane stoves, power cords, folding tables and chairs, bicycles, kayaks, weinie forks, giant cooler, smores makings, golf cart, Coleman lanterns and fuel, dishwasher and croquet set."

"Okay."

I bought a tent and already had a blowup mattress with internal pump. Nancy found my cast iron skillet, and she had a one-quart sauce pan for boiling water for instant coffee. Two pillows, two sheets, a blanket, bacon and eggs, paper plates, instant coffee, peanuts in the shell and cups. Bingo, we'd be finished, right?

But I needed a cord for the mattress pump, and she had a couple of electric lanterns, a couple of power cords for our phones, two hand flashlights, two folding chairs, a folding table, and a couple of extra pillows. We also had to have a cooler for the wine, bacon and eggs, soft drinks, half and half, and ice.

Of course, the temperatures went into the fifties, so another blanket was added. We didn't want to be glamping, but we did add two plastic wine glasses instead of drinking out of paper coffee cups like heathens.

We drove to Oscar Scherer State Park where I've volunteered for 10 years. The ranger at the ranger station said, "Hey, Joel, what are you doing here today?"

"Camping."

"Have fun."

The campsite was perfect, with natural foliage on each side and plenty of room for the tent, a car and a tennis court, because it was designed for a motorized 38-foot RV with three pullouts, an extendable canopy, and a Jeep hitched to the back. Our 10x10 tent looked sad and lonely at the back of the clearing next to a tiny close line.

The tent set up in about 10 minutes (surprise!), with only a little bit of &#@&%. I didn't even receive a welt from a Fiberglas pole snapping me in the face as had happened many times before. Back in the day, any time I went to work with a red, raised streak on my face, a colleague would smile and say: "How was camping last weekend, scout?"

Each site shared electricity and water with a neighboring site. I unpacked the mattress, plugged it in and blew it up. What I had remembered as a regular sized bed had shrunk to a twin. Oops!

I waved at the ranger on the way out and he looked surprised that we were leaving. Luckily Walmart was a mile away, and we bought a queen-sized mattress with built in pump.

I gave the ranger a military salute as we returned to the park, and he ducked his head to look into the car to see that it was really us returning so quickly.

We unpacked the mattress, and it didn't work. There was no way to plug it in. In small print on the box, it read: "Four D batteries not included." &%@#*!

NOT GLAMPING continued

After an hour of nibbling on peanuts as appetizers and throwing the shells into the fire, Nancy and I felt hungry and opened a can of Progresso creamy bean and barley soup. Trust me, I wasn't the one who picked bean and barley. The soup began boiling rapidly over the flames, and Nancy poured some steamy bumps and lumps into each of our bowls.

I lifted a spoonful toward my lips, but it never arrived. The bowl of the plastic spoon began drooping under the intense heat and deposited a scalding barleycorn on my left big toe, which was sticking out of my sandals. I did a traditional Native America dance in front of the fire while letting out war whoops.

Nancy was suppressing a laugh until she picked up her paper-plate bowl and the bottom dropped out with a soggy plop onto the picnic table. She stood there holding up and looking through a paper ring printed with miniature blue flowers. My turn to laugh, but, as the proverb goes, "he who laughs last had better not be engaged." So, I quickly looked sympathetic and said, "Oh, too bad."

The ranger didn't even look at us as we drove past the park entrance and out to the Burger King just down Tamiami Trail. I glanced at him, though, and he was wagging his head back and forth like a green, neatly uniformed bobblehead.

Back at the park, luckily, the ranger station was closed, so we didn't have another close encounter of the awkward kind. We decided it was time to turn in.

The temperature had dropped into the low 50s, so as Nancy went to the bathhouse to put on warm civilized nightclothes. I slathered a spoonful of salve on my blistered big toe and slipped on some wooly socks. I crawled onto the bed. Aaaaah! My weight made my bottom bottom out the air mattress, and a vengeful rock under the tent elbowed me in the left kidney. &%#$@!

Then I pulled up the blanket with my Polartec and convertible pants still on. I was used to backpacking, and I would never take my outer clothes off during four-day hikes in the snowy mountains of Montana.

Nancy came back into the tent dressed in cute pink and green, but heavy, PJs and socks. She stumbled on a pair of discarded boots and flopped down on the air mattress, flipping me out onto the tent floor. My! Plastic can be frigid, especially where my Polartec had scooted up to expose my bare back.

She apologized as I rolled back onto the mattress, then leaned over and said, "Good night, Hon." As she kissed my face, her ice-cold nose felt like a frozen mushroom on my cheek.

A few minutes of lying on our backs, afraid to move from the spots we had just warmed, and with the covers up to our chins, we relaxed. Aaaaah! Nancy took a deep breath, then whispered in alarm, "**What's that!**"

"What's what?" I asked, rising up on one elbow, turning my good ear toward the entrance of the tent and fumbling around for the tent stake mallet.

"That sound!"

"There's no sound."

"Oh, that's it. It's silent."

I sighed.

WHAT MAKES ME GRUMPY

I've been receiving tools that I don't need via a subscription to the Ye Ole Grumpy Warehouse tool-a-week program. Now that I'm moving to Nancy's, I realize I don't need the tools I didn't need anymore than I did before. I decided to cancel.

I went to Yeolegrumpy.com/signin, typed username ANCH, and my password, which I recalled had something to do with a pet, DOGMANGE%1.

"Your Account name or Password is incorrect."

ANCH, HAIRBALL%1. Nope!

ANCH, PARROTPOOP%1. Nope!

ANCH, FLEABAG%1. Nope!

I opted to change my password, so they sent a code by a phone message. The code flashed on the screen and then disappeared forever.

I thought I saw 81P9043M8-CARDI-B, but it wasn't accepted. I punched resend. I looked at my phone and tried to memorize a new code before it disappeared, 97J2387612-JAY-Z. No luck.

I decided I'd call them. The phone rang and the announcer said: "Welcome to Ye Ole Grumpy's front porch, please listen carefully to the menu, since it has changed recently."

I grumbled: "I bet it hasn't."

"Touch 1 to make a new subscription."

"Touch 2 to extend your subscription."

"Nope. Nyet. Nip. Not. Nada. No way."

"Touch 3 to check a delivery date."

"Nein. No-no. Huhuh. Nope."

"Touch 4 to return your order."

"Touch 5 to change your address."

"Touch 6 to rate our service."

"OMG!"

"Touch 7 to repeat this menu."

In the announcer's voice, I yelled: "Touch 8 twice firmly with a ballpeen hammer if your patience has run out."

"Touch 10 if you need to talk to customer service."

I tapped at 10 like a woodpecker.

"Hold on. Your time is important. Because of Covid 19, wait time may be longer than usual."

"Bison Chips! I bet you used to blame it on unusually high call volumes, or the computers are working slowly today."
"Click, click, bip, click, bip……"
"Oh boy, here we go."
"Thanks for holding."
"Hello, may I have names of person to whom I speaking to?"
"Joel Robbins. Who writes your scripts?"
"What the last four digits your social security numbers?"
"7192."
"And your birth of day?"
"3/7/44."
"Hold while I look your record."
"Nooo. More ticking! Is a time bomb about to go off!"
"Jo-EL, you there still?"
"Yeah. Where are you?"
"I Mumbai. How can help you today?"
"I want to cancel my subscription."
"I help you with that."
"Of course, your scripts all say that. How's the weather in India?"
"Hot, sticky and stinky. I need transfer you cancelations apartment. Please hold it."
"Wait, don't put me on hold or at least don't play…! Noooo, Bolero, the most boring, repetitive tune in the world."

………………………………………………………

"Thanks for holding, your time is important and serving you is very important to us. Remember that we have a special discount ……."
"My time important? Bull schnitzel, if you thought I was important you would hire enough people to answer the phones."
"Hello, to whom I speaking to?"
"It's still Joel Robbins."
"What's last four digits your social….?"
"It's still 7192."
"And your day of bir….?"
"It's still 3/7/44."
"What your Grumpy security code?"
"1234"
"Hold while look up record."
"Noooo! 'It's a Small World After All.' Shoot me!"

………………………………………………………..

"You still there, Jo-EL."

"Barely, and it's Joel. CANCEL ME NOW or I'm coming to Mumbai and taking some Ye Ole Grumpy rusty tools and shoving them …….."

"You sure? Mr. Grumpy will miss you."

THE QUEEN'S GATE POOL

The centerpiece of our club is a pool that reminds me of a small resort with chairs, umbrellas, palm trees, flowers and a fountain. Year round it is the gathering point of KGC people from all over the United States, but mostly Michigan. The wolverine state must be the most inhospitable place to spend the winter, that's unless you're from New England, where they wear those bulbous, white Mickey Mouse boots during the summer, or the frost-bitten-nose capital of the US, Minnesota.

Pool conversations can be unusual for several reasons. Take this one for example:

"Hey, that you, Joel? Didn't recognize you with your clothes off."

"What?"

Or.

"Joel, I'll show you mine if you'll show me yours."

"You'd better be talking about scars, Rod."

Or.

"Hey, John, the rule is organ recitals can only last 10 minutes."

"What! I could spend 20 just on my gall bladder."

One of the other main pool topics concerns eating out. Wives have carried the burden of planning meals, grocery shopping and cooking for 50+ years by the time they come to QGC. They've had it. So:

"Where's the best place for pizza? "

"Bogey's, Frankie's, Benny's Bada Bing, Valenti's, Joey D's, Hungry Howie's, Mama Leone's, or any other Italian place with a word ending in E, I, IE or sometimes Y. I learned that in grammar class. A, E, I, O, U and sometimes Y.

Other popular topics include how to cure toenail fungus, how to tweeze nose and earhole hair, how to keep the chlorine water from melting your swimwear (especially while you're in the pool," how your friend manages to throw his numerous empty beer, wine, whiskey and other liquor bottles into the recycle bin without anyone thinking he's a lush, or how to shave a bald spot without having to use a styptic pencil or shred of toilet paper to staunch the blood from a nick.

The pool is used only for "women-only" water exercising five days a week. Some of those days, I pretend to be cross gender and join them. I've a habit of doing a sissy scream if the water's chilly, which warns the women to be prepared for when the water rises to the upper sensitive areas of their anatomy. Now, even when the water system is haywire, making the water feeling more like a hot tub than a refreshing lake, I still have to scream, or they think I'm in trouble with Nancy for not putting the trash, refuge, recyclables, hazardous waste, kiosk goods, garbage and broken concrete edging in the correct receptable, shed, bin. etc. Yes, I get confused.

Anyway, I don't like the 2+ hour exercises on Tuesday and Thursdays, so I go late and leave early. When I arrive 30 minutes late, I wave at all the girls and say, "Can we start over."

A chorus of noes is the answer.

When a section ends with the lady on the tape saying, "That was wonderful. See you next time."

I yell, "Great, it's over," and start for the ladder out of the pool.

"No, Joel, there's two more sections."

I stay a little longer, then when they're all facing the edge of the pool in a new exercise, I sneak through the middle without them noticing. If one catches me, I just say: "It's about 11, gotta go. Nap time."

RECAPTURING MY CHILDHOOD WITH SHARP OBJECTS

Remember when you were a kid? I can remember then sometimes better than I can remember now, for example, where my cell phone is. I used to hunt with a .410 shotgun and a .22 Rifle, shoot plastic toy soldiers with my BB gun, stick frogs with a forked spear and shoot gar and shad with my bow and arrow. The old cotton wood trees in our farm's fence rows were not safe from being stabbed and splintered from our camp knife throwing.

A neighbor farm boy and I made a mini-cannon using a wagon tongue, cinnamon balls, firecrackers and a brick. The barn wasn't safe from our candy barrage. We used soy beans and large straws as pea shooters, then darts from our dart board to menace pigeons in a hay barn. The birds were safe from our developing junior high large- and fine-motor skills.

I remember when we played Mumblety-peg (also known as mumbley-peg, mumblepeg, mumble-the-peg, mumbledepeg, mumble-de-peg or root-a-peg)? It required a two-bladed folding pocketknife. From a sitting position with legs apart, the object was to throw it so that it landed and stuck in different positions—over your head, behind your back, a double flip, one blade in the ground, two blades stuck, a two-finger throw, a palm throw, and throws starting from your forehead, nose, ears and mouth. Contestants progressed through the many challenges and had to stop when they didn't succeed. Then the other contestant picked up from he had left off during his turn. The first one through all the challenges won.

Then there was Split the Kipper, or simply Splits. The object was to stand facing your best friend about three feet apart and throw a knife at his feet. Well, not exactly at, but near his feet. You started with your feet about a foot apart and took turns throwing a knife within a couple of inches of one of your friend's feet. It had to stick or it didn't count. Then he had to move his foot to touch the knife, pull it out of the ground and throw it at your feet. Eventually one competitor was so stretched out, or split, that he couldn't keep his balance and fell over. It was wise to wear leather shoes rather than sandals for this game.

My first few years at KGC, I found myself batting a felt covered rubber ball back and forth across a net, sliding a black or yellow ceramic disk down a concrete course toward a triangular target, playing frisbee golf or throwing bags of corn at a hole in a box. The child daredevil in me was thoroughly ashamed.

So, lately Nancy and I have been shooting BB guns at leaves floating down Salt Creek or tin cans on a box or the empty plastic bears that honey comes in. It's somehow satisfying.

The other day I invited Rod and Lucy over to compete in a blowgun competition. They accepted and Rod, only Rod in all of King's Gate Club, would have his own blowguns and darts. We shot from sitting positions in Nancy's carport and our aim was lethal to ferocious-looking, inflated red, blue, orange, yellow and green balloons. One of the neighbor ladies came out of her house, looked at four seniors puffing on blowguns to send needle-sharp darts flying through the air. She decided it was not a good time to bend over and pull weeds in her flower beds.

When the sky darkened, Rod and I tried a little axe throwing. I have a regular camp hatchet and a special axe for competitive throwing. It's kind of a cross between a long-handled axe and a hatchet. I had made an end-grained wooden target, which I sat on a wooden chair.

BAM. From twelve feet the axe struck the target in the middle and stuck with such force that the chair went tumbling and the target flying. Lucy yelled, "JOEL, what did you do!" Now this is a man's sport, I thought. Rod tried the camp hatchet, but it just bounced off the target. Then he tried the throwing axe and split the seat of the chair. YES! This beats throwing bags of dried lima beans at a hole.

I also have throwing knives, but I didn't bring them out. Nancy has a wild arm, and the first time she threw one, the knife went way over the top of the target and into the bushes in the five acres, never to be seen again.

HOEING OUT MY HOUSE

Getting my house ready to sell was a chore for both Nancy and me. I remember starting on kitchen drawers. I attached a hose onto the sweeper, left the can opener, an assortment of serving forks and spoons, a potato masher, wooden chopsticks, dozens of toothpicks, and a cheese slicer in the drawer, then vacuumed, shaking the drawer to move the utensils around. When all toast crumbs and other dust and coffee grounds didn't come out, I put the hose on the sweeper exhaust and blew the toothpicks and debris into the air and onto the floor to sweep up later. Aaahh. Done with that drawer.

Then I looked over at Nancy on her knees cleaning other kitchen drawers. She took all the utensils out, washed and dried them, wiped the dust and crumbs out with a wet rag, dried it with a clean towel, then cut and inserted marble-patterned shelf liner. I knew right then and there my method wasn't going to fly.

While she continued to clean and line, I discovered a rubber ball in one drawer and used the pressure from the vacuum hose to suspend it in midair. I was grinning like a monkey catching peanuts at the zoo.

"Look, Nancy. Magic." She wasn't amused.

The drawers done, we moved on to the pictures on the walls. Sara's art we kept, but some prints Sara liked that I never could stand. I started to throw one into the trash pile.

"Don't throw that away, Joel. I love pink flamingos," Nancy said.

"Where would you put it?"

"In your office/guest room at my house."

Just then I "tripped," tossed the picture so that it landed on the corner of the frame. The frame accordioned and split. I lurched forward off balance and "accidently" put my foot through the middle of the print.

"Oops, I guess we'll have to discard it after all."

Nancy was excited about staging the house. She traded lamps and furniture from her house that looked better in mind. She did a great job. Then pillows started to procreate. Seven on the sofa, eight on the trundle bed, four on the twin bed and six on the queen.

I was afraid to open a closet for fear that a horde of newly hatched pillows would come billowing out, stampede, overwhelm me and suffocate me

Some had messages on them—"Salt Life," "Surf's Up," "Joel's Napping," "Relax You're Retired," "Your Text Here" (that was a free sample), "Pray, Eat, Love," "Get Cozy," and "Irony Is the Opposite of Wrinkly."

When we were finished removing 50% of the shelves, storage containers and furniture, Nancy said, "This looks great! Maybe we should move here and sell mine. We could hoe out my house."

Yes, Nancy Brown, a Connecticut girl, used "hoe out." I was afraid to comment on a phrase that contained the word "hoe."

I did yell: "Noooo! That would mean starting all over "hoeing out" YOUR house.

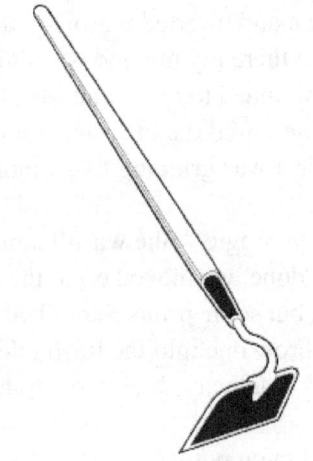

IT FINALLY HAPPENED

Women are "nesters." Sara added furniture or moved pieces around for no apparent reason other than the joy of rearranging feathers in HER nest. My nest? The shed. My feathers? Tools. I have several gnarly toes from stubbing them on a moved table while walking droopy-eyed to the living room at night to investigate a sound only Sara had heard.

When Nancy and I moved in together, she feathered her nest with lots of my furniture and Sara's paintings. So, once settled, I felt at home. She gave me the guest bathroom and office space in the adjoining bedroom. My clothes were in that closet, shoes on a rack. I put up hooks for visors, hats, lounging shorts, work clothes, beach towels and belts.

Sure, she put my socks in the top drawer and my boxers in the bottom, whereas I had put my socks in the second drawer and my boxers in the top. Men are a little slow adapting, so it took me six and half weeks to acclimate. Luckily, she wasn't realigning the furniture every week.

Then it happened! I came home from the pool one afternoon, and the world had changed. My stuff had been switched with stuff from HER bathroom. As a man, I was completely discombobulated. We guys need matters simple.

Nancy said the new arrangement would work better. She noticed my eyes were crossed, so she said, "Let's just try it, Honey." My brain was screaming "NOOO!" But, okay, I hung my beach towel and wet swim trunks on hooks in what had been her bathroom.

Now I had to go to what had been her closet off the master bedroom for my clothes. After I changed, I grabbed my gray slip-on Sketchers. I could only get four toes in, my pinky toe hung out. With palpitations, I looked to see if my ankles and feet had swollen. Nope. Then I realized that the Sketchers had pink stitching. &%#@&. The shoe racks hadn't been switched.

Before I got acclimated, I started one day by taking her Centrum, calcium, serotonin, baby aspirin and iron pills from the bottles lined up on the windowsill in my old bathroom instead of my regular blood pressure, acetaminophen, cholesterol, probiotic and antacid pills.

Then I took a shower, and I came away smelling NOT like Head and Shoulders "Ole Spice for Ole Men" but "Jasmine Dancing in Spring Time" parfum. In the woodshop, friend Chuck gave one sniff and backed away from me like I was a rattlesnake.

When I donned my light blue "SEA LIFE" visor, it perched on my bean like a pint-sized aluminum saucepan. Yep, I discovered more pink stitching instead of navy blue.

I wanted revenge. She was tooling around in the golf cart on errands, so I decided to adjust the visor strap to the largest setting, so when she put it on it would fall to around her neck like a horse collar. I chuckled at the image.

But instead, I went to the kitchen and switched the silverware drawer with the hot pad/dishcloth drawer, and the corkscrew, can opener, garlic squeezer and potato masher drawer with the spoons, ladles, knives and spatulas drawer.

Then I switched the dinner plates with the coffee cups in the cupboard. I emptied the flour and sugar from their containers into big bowls and then poured them into the opposite canisters. "How do you like them bananas, Nancy!"

Then I started feeling guilty and hurriedly put everything back before she caught me being a lowlife, vindictive doofus. She flashed through the door just as I was finishing and asked why I was sweating. She had taken tea with neighbor Phyllis and went to brush any stains from her teeth.

She came out looking sheepish: "I just used your toothbrush by mistake--Yuk! And I wiped my mouth on your wet swim trunks--Yikes! You hung your trunks where I usually have my hand towel." I hid a grin.

The next day all my stuff was magically back in the guest bathroom and hers in the master bath. Peace and tranquility reigned again.

MALE EGO

All men want to be superheroes, and I grew up idolizing cowboy-in-white Hopalong Cassidy, and also hero Audie Murphy, WW II hero. The best plotline for movies and books, according to males my age, must include "men with guns going somewhere to do something dangerous." That line is from <u>Bless the Beasts and the Children</u>.

A shooting range, Total Defense 007, is right next to an Ace Hardware I frequent. I thought it would be fun to go over and shoot some bad guys. My name? Bond, JOEL Bond.

I don't hunt, I don't carry a murder weapon and I wasn't in the military. In fact, I was in the Peace Corps in my 60s. We volunteers were deployed around the world to create good will and a friendly and harmonious image of America and Americans. Carrying a revolver wouldn't have sent the correct message to the people I worked with for two and a half years in Azerbaijan.

But, I still have male DNA. So, the other day I embarrassed myself by going to the 007 shooting range. I asked the young girl behind the desk for a loaner pistol, thinking a Colt .45 Lone Ranger revolver with pearl white grips. She handed me two gun cases, one a Glock 9 mm and the other an S&W 22 lr, both semi-automatics.

She made me sign my car, house and life away before going to the range. This petit blonde read me 78 rules, and I was afraid there would be a test at the end. Then she asked, "Do you have eyes and ears." I hadn't looked in a mirror for an hour or so, but I assumed so and replied, "Yes."

She assigned me lane 5. I started to open the range door when she said I had to have eyes and ears on before entering; she held up tinted glasses and ear protection. I showed her my plastic carpenter's earmuffs, acted like "I knew that." She gave me the "sure!" look and loaned me glasses. If you're wondering, yes, they're called earmuffs. Feeling like I had on Mickey Mouse ears that muffled sounds as if I were under water, I walked onto the range. There were metal spring clips on a piece of cardboard for attaching a target. I went back out, took off my mouse ears and bought a target, a dirty one. That doesn't mean muddy or one with smutty girlie pictures, it has special paint that cracks off when hit by a bullet. That makes it easier to see bullet holes from a distance. The blonde grinned and winked. Well, it was not actually a wink, more like closing one eye for two seconds and glaring with the other.

I started to load my S&W 22lr and realized the case contained no bullets. I left the range and went back to the blonde, whose eyebrows were raised, implying, "Who is this old dude?" Probably thinking she'd run into a modern-day Barney Fife, Don Quixote or Walter Mitty. No, she was too young to know those characters. Shoulders slumped, I bought one box of shells and slogged back to the range.

I pushed every lever on the gun but couldn't get the magazine to release. I looked through the window at the blonde, and she signaled me with an index finger—be there in one second. When she arrived, she deftly flicked a lever and, bingo, out it came. I wanted to tell her that in my youth I was able to open a beer bottle with my teeth and a pickle jar with my bare hands.

Then, anticipating my next blunder, she opened the ammo box and loaded a few rounds into the clip. She lifted one of my earmuffs and said: "See?"

I clipped on the target, which was two feet away. That made it easy to hit the bullseye 10 times in a row. When I proudly turned around to toss the brass empties in a bucket, knowing that I could use the target as a trophy to prove my gun-handling prowess to fiancée Nancy, I looked up and saw the blonde watching through the range window and motioning toward the end of the range, then at the wall to my left. I was caught. There was a toggle switch, which, when I pushed it forward, sent the target racing on a bicycle chain to the other end of the building. I nodded and she nodded.

I shot another clip of 22s at the target. Then I toggled the switch to bring the target back for viewing. I had missed everything. Well, I did blow one of the spring clips off the edge of the target holder. Yep, she saw! I turned around and shrugged at the window. She looked away and shook her head.

For my own self pride, the 9mm pistol box stayed closed, because I knew it also wouldn't have ammunition for it, and I didn't want to wear out the young girl's eyebrows.

REPLACING A FANNY

   Some of you know that I'm baching it at Nancy's this week. Pray for me. I'm in the process of washing a batch of clothes. How do you spell batch-e-lor? I was used to my washer and dryer at my house, but not Nancy's. So, I dumped all the clothes into her washer and threw in a couple of handfuls of purple soap pods, five or six, closed my eyes and twiddled each dial before punching the START button.
   Why didn't I wait for Nancy to come back? My clothes hamper was billowing over like warm root beer poured over a glass full of ice cream. Plus, the bedroom was beginning to smell like the insole of my tennis sneakers wrapped in the armpit of one of my sweaty T-shirts.
   The kitchen went to pot the first day, and, being a romantic guy, I sent a photo of it to Nancy so she could see how much I was missing her.
   When I stopped by Rae Burmaster's for a visit, she asked how I was keeping busy with my fiancée gone for more than a week.
   Well, I told her that a box had been sitting in the middle of the living room for a week before she left. It takes a while, but I can home in on a hint. Sara was always surprised when the recyclables and trash sat at the door for a few days before I figured out that I was supposed to take corrective action.
   Anyway, just before she left, I asked about the box.
MISTAKE.
   "I want the chandelier taken down, because there is no longer a table under it," she said.
   "There might be later, though," I countered.
   Ignoring my dodge, she continued: "And I want the fan taken down and moved to David's house, then replace it with the fan in the box."
   "Let me get this clear, you want me to take down a working fan and replace it with a fan."
   "This one has a light in it. You don't have to do it if you don't want to," she commented as she gave me a sweet smile.
   I was sunk.
   So, I spent yesterday proverbially digging a hole and filling it in. Then digging another hole and filling it in with fancier dirt. Then delivering the dirt to David's. Please, don't let Nancy see this.

The chandelier had more cutglass hanging from it than the entire collection of England's Crown Jewels. But, I got it down without cutting myself or breaking any of the sparklies.

The fan was from Arkansas Hill Inc., so, of course, it was made in China. Mysteriously, they let a Mandarin [我认为是这样的] with an English dictionary and a QWERTY keyboard prepare the directions and list of parts.

The box only contained 94 pieces. I did my own translation of the parts list: fan housing, light kit, glass bowl, bulb, pull chain and red fabric lock washer were listed as a fanny housing, light kite, a glass bowel, a blub, a pull chair and a read blade washer and dryer.

I tried the Spanish version of the directions with no luck. A "tornillo vamoose aspa" sounded like, "run from the little tornado ASP."

Tools were not included, and I had to use two electric screw drivers; a lineman's pliers; needle nose pliers; a hammer; a shim; a magnet for searching the rug for tiny, dropped bolts; a rainbow assortment of wire nuts (#10, #12, #14, # 16, #18, #20); black electrician's tape; two screwdrivers, Phillips and slotted; adhesive putty to keep the tiny screws on my screwdriver; a ladder; white touchup paint; and a Valium.

Anyway, I finished the project with only nine extra pieces that I hid from Nancy behind some doilies in a drawer.

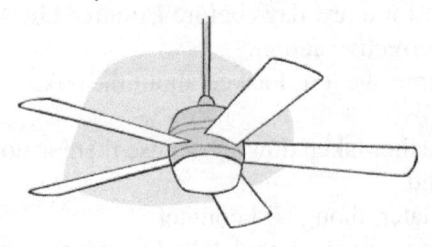

WHERE'S MY COLLATERAL?

What do you do with a little extra money in this economy? There's real estate, for one. That's where you get a patch of land that you can live on, raise an animal on or grow food on. So, if you have a tent, a rabbit, a carrot, water and an onion, you can at least eat soup in your own abode.

Then there's unreal estate. That's where you buy stock or bond certificates that list how many shares of a business you own. That's it! There's not enough paper certificates to keep your head dry in a rainstorm. And if you're dying of hunger, you can boil them all day, add salt and pepper, eat them and you'll still go ahead and die.

One time I had $45,000 I wanted to add to my nest egg with the hope of also making a little money. I didn't want more property to care for, so, I talked to a financial advisor at a bank I use. He mentioned saving's accounts, stocks, bonds, certificates of deposit (CDs), and mutual funds.

I wanted my money protected, so I asked for specifics about each product.

He told me stocks and bonds were not protected, so a mismanaged company can default (as GM did), leaving $100,000 worth of your stocks worthless, barely useful for blotting your new puppy's latest piddle puddle.

Saving's accounts were guaranteed by FDIC up to a couple hundred thousand but paid only one tenth of one percent (1 mil) interest. I might as well bury the money in my petunia patch.

CDs were insured too, but they only paid one half of a percent (half a penny) interest. Maybe I'd be better burying it under a begonia bush.

That left mutual funds. They can also go squat, but since the potential disaster is spread over multiple "excellent" companies, your outright panic is reduced to an under-the-surface constant gnawing angst about your nested eggs.

I reminded the Ameribrite advisor that his company always had poster, newspaper and TV ads that encouraged car and house buyers to give Ameribrite money so that it could make more money for itself. I continued by saying now the situation was reversed. I had money that I wanted to give to his company so I could make more money. He was all eyes and big ears.

"When I took your money, you required my house title as collateral, so now that you're taking my money, I want something real as collateral too."

His eyes narrowed and his ears shrunk. Your company protects itself in case I don't make you a lot of money or no money at all, and now I want to protect myself in case you don't do a good job with my nest of eggs and the stocks and bonds in the mutual funds fail.

There was a lot of silence, then the advisor excused himself to use the loo. I saw him enter his boss's office, sit and talk, talk, talk before he returned with his eyes brighter, his "tinkling" supposedly done.

"We don't offer collateral because mutual funds in the long run never fail," he offered.

"I'm almost 80, so I don't have a 'long run, sir.' And, if they never fail, you can give me a guarantee backed by the assets of Ameribrite." I countered.

His pretend bladder problem flared up again.

The "tinkle, tinkle, tinkle" was their voices and took place not in the loo but in his boss's office again.

I took the opportunity to walk out the door with my $45,000 and go to a dealer in tangibles that have intrinsic value, gold and silver.

A LIFE OF CONTINUAL DIETING

Why aren't any diets one and out. I've tried them all, they all work, until you go off them. I remember when I was a high schooler I would fill a giant tumbler with ice cream, real ice cream that was a diary product—milk and cream—not water, tofu and artificial vanilla. I'd melt a Hershey's chocolate bar and pour it on top. I didn't gain a gram.

There were side effects, though. I didn't break out with ruby red, angry spots all over my forehead, I just had one pimple the size and shape of a pinkish chocolate chip with a white volcanic tip. It usually found a place on my nose to grow roots, and lasted weeks, especially if there was a school dance or prom coming up.

Diet has a troubling name. Die, which mean die, and et, which means small, like dinette or spinet. So together we have little death, which is about how I feel each time I have to pass up a bacon, cheese hamburger with pickles, mustard, deep fried onions and ketchup for a grilled chicken salad where the chicken tastes exactly like chicken. Nobody seems to eat chicken without catsup, barbecue sauce, deep fried cornmeal breading, or butter and blue cheese (cordon bleu).

Speaking of hamburgers, recently, I decided to splurge and eat the aorta clogging burger above, then go the next day to the workout room. There I could pedal my heart out and erase the globs of fat I had added to my waist. The burger calorie count came to 917 and my hour workout at a 10-mph level only made up 212 measly calories.

One time Sara and I were on a surefire diet, and about 4:15 pm after school I was already hanging out in the kitchen hoping a hot cheesy, pepperoni pizza would leap out of the oven. Sara came in to ask why my head was lying on the second shelf of the refrigerator. I told her I was famished, because I had had only a slice of cheese on melba toast all day and my stomach was making noises like a lion cub wanting to suckle.

"What are we having for dinner," I asked.

"Split pea soup."

"We're cutting back on calories so much that we're splitting peas!"

"Here's a couple of stalks of celery to hold you until supper."

I googled the nutritional value of celery and found that it's 103% water and -3% of a mysterious, fibrous substance. It not only had no taste, it had no nutritional value either. So, I handed the stalks back to Sara and drank a glass of water and swallowed a Metamucil 4-in-1 fiber tablet. That saved me from jawing celery for fifteen minutes followed by spitting out a ball of string, which was probably that mysterious fiber

    Nancy and I don't diet, but we try to be careful. She's better than I am. When it hits 8:34 in the evening, I begin grazing on anything I don't have to cook, starting in the top shelf of the cabinets and working my way down through drawers to the bottom shelf of the refrigerator. I stop when I get to the celery in the crisper.

A SIMPLE SOUTH AMERICAN WEDDING

By September 2021, Nancy and I had been living together for several months. That arrangement is common but I wanted something else. We had booked a trip to Croatia, and I didn't fancy calling Nancy my "girlfriend." She's in her sixties and I'm in my seventies! We're not teenagers giving each other class rings with pink angora wrapped around the boy's and the girl's on a stainless steel lavalier. "Significant other" sounds like a cousin; "partner" sounds like we're part of an LLC; and "roommate" sounds like we're shacking up while attending college.

So, I asked Nancy to marry me. Whoa! That opened a Pandora's box, or can of worms, to mix metaphors. Still, I gave her a ring and we had a smooth time using fiancée and fiancé on our Adriatic trip. But back in Nokomis, the questions were who, when, where, why and how are you going to get married. I felt like I was back advising a newspaper staff where the keys to reporting were finding the 5Ws and the H.

OMG! Nancy wanted her 4 children, 6 siblings, their spouses, her mother, some of their assorted canines, felines and hircine and all members of King's Gate Club to attend. Sara and I had eloped. I'm being facetious. I only wanted Nancy and me.

We checked with everyone but the pets and King's Gators (sic), and they were fine with not being there. That's how I feel about most people's marriages. I'm happy they're wedding, I just don't want to watch it happen. That could be a man thing, or a Joel thing. She still wanted others there. I still wanted only Nancy and me and maybe my cat Blue.

We realized, if we started trying to set a date that would work for everyone it wouldn't work great for anyone. Those on the list were tied up on certain dates, others had work schedules, holidays were coming, and we were going to Patagonia the first of October. Now I realize why there are so many June brides and winter bachelors.

Idea! Get married in Patagonia. She said with a loving smile that then our honeymoon would be in Argentina and Chile. Things were looking up for not having a $30,000 wedding and all that would entail. She was still worried about a wedding dress, shoes, rings, preacher, chapel, bridesmaid, best man, flowers, candles, cake, rice, venue, champagne, rehearsals, reception dinner, a tuxedo, my shoes, my shirt, mani- and pedi-cures, facials, photos and whatnot. Silly me, I was thinking we didn't need any of those. I voted for hiking boots, cargo pants, parkas, two cupcakes and beer. I just wanted it over so I could enjoy the "wilderness at the end of the world" with my love.

I said we could be married by the captain of the trip's expedition ship while sailing up the fjords of Chile. "Doesn't that sound romantic," I said.

We called our trip leader in Calafate, Argentina, and Elisa Rodriguez Giglio said she knew of a priest and a chapel in her village. That also sounded romantic. The captain said he'd try to work a wedding in, but the priest said the Santa Teresita festival was at that time.

When we were down to one week, packing for staging a wedding, hiking mountains in possible rain and snow, viewing glaciers while braving stormy seas, and dining in upscale Buenos Aires restaurants, became an Argentine Airlines weight-limit issue.

To make a long story short--I know, too late--we were too "wedding" anxious to wait for the cruise part of the trip, so, we shopped for champagne, flowers and a *dulce de leche* white cake covered in peanuts. We felt like locals. Then we met in the Recoleta Arc Hotel meeting room with our trip leader and fellow travelers for orientation. After that, we announced: "Surprise, we were getting married right now."

Nancy wore a gorgeous lacey, Spanish looking, dark blue dress, and I had on a black turtleneck and gray sport coat.

David Eddy, Nancy's brother, was on the trip too and agreed to be our "officiant." We said our "I do's," exchanged rings and kissed. Our new fellow travelers signed our marriage certificate as witnesses," we popped the cork, drank toasts, ate cake, and Nancy threw the bouquet. Then we climbed to the eleventh-floor terrace, took pictures overlooking Buenos Aires and shared a dinner of empanadas at a local restaurant with the Eddys. Nothing to it! *Muy marvilloso*!

EMPTYING MY HOUSE AND SELLING IT

At the end of the session with an attorney working on the closing on my house in King's Gate Club, the new owners asked, "Is there anything else you want from the house?"

When I stopped by the last time, the soon-to-be owners told me I had clothes and some small boxes in a couple of bedroom drawers. Now I know what happened to my lounging shorts, a couple of T-shirts, a Venice, Florida, visor, and some boxers that Nancy thought she had left at the laundromat after Ian ruined her washer and dryer.

My kids Kristin and Mason had gone through the house to take what they wanted or needed for their homes. Nancy and I had moved tons of things to her house. So, I thought, no, nothing else.

Then my mind ran a "video disc" backward over the past 10 years, and I thought

There's got to be a pretzel, bits of popcorn, a few M&Ms and a very, very dry handful of puckered raisins, and a pound or so of roasted peanuts between the pads in the sofa. No, don't need them, bought a fresh jar of Planters the other day.

Then there was that 10-cent ring I had spent seven dollars and seventy-five cents in quarters on. My masculinity had been challenged at a street fair booth, where winning jewelry involved swinging a giant mallet that sent a weight shooting up a post to ring a bell and a pain shooting down to inflame my sciatica. One night Nancy had been spinning the ring on the coffee table when it sprung away, twirled across the floor and executed a rattling cannonball down one of the air ducts. I'd like to see that again.

Of course, the air vents have always acted as magnets, attracting every finish nail, tap screw, tiny washer, lock nut, and other small pieces of metal from ceiling fans, table lamps, grandchildren's toys, picture frames and shelving that was being assembled or repaired. Those would probably fill a nice gherkin jar with hardware.

Any day I was expecting a landslide of coffee grounds to start avalanching out from between the stove and the counters at the house I was selling. When Sara was not looking, it was much neater to palm the coffee into the crack than to the edge of the counter where it eventually dodged my hand or dishcloth and waterfalled onto the floor.

I told the soon-to-be owners that one day the washing machine would regurgitate a matching purple, tan, and red argyle sock it had swallowed last year. Its mate looks lonely in my sock drawer.

Each time I shaved, about three times a week, I dropped a penny in the slot in the back of the medicine cabinet. Well, I didn't have separate razor blades to put in there, so it was my piggy bank. Someday it'll be a nice treasure chest of copper.

I thought of all the replacement Christmas twinkle-light bulbs and their weeny fuses that must have spilled out from behind the Fibber McGee "drawer," down behind the other drawers beneath them, and finally onto the floor for a reunion of holiday trash "survivors."

And Wiggles, my friendly ball python, that got away last month. I'd take him back. We liked him, even though we didn't relish reaching under the bed to extract him from his favorite hiding place. He kept us alert because he would crawl under the sheets in the morning to warm up. Nancy would feel him cross her shoulder then turn to me: "Later, honey."

Seriously, thinking about it, now that I have my underwear back, there's nothing else I really need, so it's all theirs.

Note: As with most of my Bill Bryson-type tales, much of the content is fabricated. So don't think I stuffed coffee grounds between the cabinets, I just often wanted to. Plus, there's no Wiggles, thankfully. After one post, a lady came up to me and told me that pesto, which I had found in my pantry, was not fish food made of ground grass and flies. I didn't tell her that I knew that, because it made a good joke to act as if I didn't. If you aren't old enough to know who Fibber McGee is, google Throckmorton P. Gildersleeve and "closet" together.

About the Author

Joel Robbins is a retired high school English and journalism teacher and a retired journalist. He grew up in the Midwest, living in Ohio, Indiana and Kentucky. He served two and a half years in Azerbaijan in the Peace Corps, where he taught English as a foreign language to future Azeri English teachers. He is married to Nancy Eddy Brown, and has two children by his marriage to the deceased Sara Stoops and four grandchildren. He now lives in Florida.

Other books by Robbins are *InGear: Peace Corps & Beyond, Ursa Caucasia, Ersatz News, Welsh Pears* and *Appalachian Tales*.